TALES
OF
FIRENZUOLA

TALES

OF

FIRENZUOLA

TRANSLATED
ANONYMOUSLY

*

SECOND EDITION
WITH AN INTRODUCTION
AND BIBLIOGRAPHY
BY
EILEEN GARDINER

ITALICA PRESS
NEW YORK
1987

First Published Privately 1889
Isidore Liseux
Paris

*

Private Reprint Edition
Copyright © 1929 by the Firenzuola Society
New York

*

Second Edition
Copyright © 1987 by Italica Press

ITALICA PRESS, INC.
595 Main Street
New York, New York 10044

Library of Congress Cataloging-in-Publication Data

Firenzuola, Agnolo, 1493-1543.
    Tales of Firenzuola.

    Bibliography: p.
    Contents: The handsome slave -- The metamorphosis -- The double change -- [etc.]
    I. Gardiner, Eileen. II. Title.
PQ4622.A2   1987   853'.3   86-82698
ISBN 0-934977-04-6 (pbk.)

Printed in the United States of America
5 4 3 2

CONTENTS

ILLUSTRATIONS

PREFACE

This edition of *The Tales of Firenzuola* or *I ragionamenti* by Agnolo Firenzuola (1493-1543) is a slight moderni - zation of the translation into English from Italian that first was published in 1889 by Isidore Liseux in Paris and reprinted in New York in 1929. The translator is anonymous but believed to be English. The translation was accompanied by a Preface, which is reprinted here.

This edition includes a bibliography of Firenzuola's works, their English translations and the most significant Italian studies. There have not been any full-length studies published in English. In fact, this bibliography is believed to be the first one available to a general English-speaking audience. Until now Agnolo Firenzuola has remained virtually unknown to American readers. It is our hope that this edition will help to change this situation.

*

INTRODUCTION

The *Tales of Firenzuola* are delightful pictures of Tuscany during the Renaissance. This was a world of wealthy merchants, handsome youths and pretty women, of lusty nuns and lecherous and greedy priests. The *Tales* are probably the most popular of Agnolo Firenzuola's prose works. On one side they continued in the popular Boccacian story-telling tradition, and on the other side the *Tales* contain the seeds of the developing Italian novel of the sixteenth century.

The *Tales* were originally conceived as a cycle of 36 tales to be told over six days by three gentlemen and three ladies. The discourse on the nature of love, which was intended as an introduction or frame to the cycle of *Tales,* was completed; but it is not considered a successful piece. The *Tales* that were completed include the six that were supposed to be included in the first day and several that were intended as part of the storytelling of later days.

The *Tales* are humorous and realistic pictures of a secular urban life. There is only one story, "The Handsome Slave," that recalls the courtly style of the Middle Ages. Despite the wife-stealing and the husband-deceiving that goes on, the husband is a "pagan" and the wife converts to Christianity, so it is essentially a tale of enobling love.

By contrast, the other tales reflect the worldly realism of the town rather than the elevated idealism of the court. In five of the *Tales* the plot revolves around the attempts of the characters to fulfill some sexual goal. This sexuality is treated with good humor, and in these tales sexuality is not necessarily synonymous with deceit or lechery. In other words, these are not really moral tales. "The Metamorphosis" is a January/May tale, where the young girl, Lavinia, is happily able to fulfill her natural sexual inclinations when a young man, aided by Fortune and having similar inclinations, poses as a maid in her old husband's house. In "The Double Change" an extremely attractive and capable Agnoletta engineers, for the sake of some extra-marital activity, an affair with an Abbot. Although the man who subsequently visits when her husband is away is not the abbot, and he is not sleeping with the maid, as he had intended, neither of them are the wiser and both are much happier. "The Temptation of the Flesh" descibes how nuns can compensate for their unmarried state in a world where the want of a dowry, rather than religious devotion, often leads to the convent. "The Even Match" tells of a widowed mother who is satisfied by the attentions of a local priest and her unmarried daughter by the attentions of the local lawyer.

Just as these *Tales* are without the moral tone of medieval tales, they also are without the misogyny that characterizes earlier *Tales*. Women are portrayed as naturally sexual and clever people. Although they often use their cleverness to fool a senile husband or gain some extra money, they are not portrayed as unusually mali - cious or a danger to virtuous men. The tellers pass no judgement on any of these men or women or their exploits unless, of course, the character happens to be a priest.

Firenzuola, a monk himself, seems to delight in taking aim at clerics, and the *Tales* are characterized by a considerable degree of anticlericalism. Priests and monks are generally portrayed as a lecherous or greedy men. Presumably vowed to chastity and poverty, they can hardly be characterized as chaste or poor. Rather than withdrawing into their own world, they try to bridge into a sexual and mercantile world where they have no place. Time and again Firenzuola shows them in this light. In "The Penance," a wonderful tale of revenge, the priest is both lecherous and stingy, so while he succeeds in gaining a pretty lover, through his meanness he manages to lose her and considerably more besides. Another tale of revenge, "The Will," tells of a widow who is pursued by a monk for her money. Her sons, however, manage to save their inheritance and make a fool of the cleric. In this tale, Firenzuola digresses from his story to deliver an explicit attack on the gluttony, luxury and treachery of the clerical life.

While sex, money and revenge all play a part in the remaining three tales, they are slightly more complex. "The Sewed-Up Bride" is definitely among the bawdiest of the *Tales,* but the tale is one of trickery. Monna Mechera, the mother of the bride, is after the dowry that has been offered to her daughter by a wealthy Florentine merchant as thanks for a favor gained through the intercession of the Cross. The prospective husband has gone off on an overextended business trip, thus placing the money temporarily out of reach. The daughter and their neighbor, who pretends to be her husband in order to get the dowry, carry their pretend marriage to its logical conclusion. Until the real husband returns, these two carry on their affair, with the mother's consent, since "one does not soil the trough more to make ten loaves than one." In the end the neighbor is without the bride or the money, but the narrator tells us, "he who possesses once for all does not always suffer."

In "The Two Friends" there is love and revenge, and there is also murder and punishment, but the story is essentially about the faithful friend who, despite affronts and rebukes, is the one who can be relied on when summoned. The story is complex, with several turns of plot. It could serve as a synopsis for a full-length novel where many twists and turns conspire to bring about the ultimate fate of the main character, Niccolo degli Albizi, and his friend Lapo.

Finally, "The Precious Jewel" is a story of trickery, where the clever man who plans the trick ends up by being tricked by an even more clever young girl. In this story there is a great deal of attention given to the development of the main character, Santolo. He is not physically described, as most of the characters are, but his character and pesonality are carefully developed. He is not a stock character, like Cecc' Antonio Fornari, the January of "The Metamorphosis," but an individual that the author has drawn so that we easily recognize the effects of this joke on his somewhat complex character.

Quite a bit has been written on the highly mature and developed style of Italian prose evident in Firenzuola's work. In this small selection it is possible to see an author with a great deal of control over this element. The style of the individual *Tales* varies with the type of story. In

"The Handsome Slave," for instance, there is a great deal of the internal deliberation that goes with the slower pace of the courtly genre. "The Penance," probably the most vicious of the stories, is full of fast dialog and quick action, until the final moments of the story when our priest, Dom Caprone, is given a chance to think over his life. By contrast with the rest of the story this is a long, slow and painful ending, as it is surely meant to be. In the bawdy tales especially, Firenzuola is magnificently adept at the quick dialog, the cutting altercation and the colloquial expression, which bring with them a taste of sharp realism. This style is evident in the arguments between Monna Francesca and her daughter in "The Even Match" and Lavinia and her husband in "The Metamorphosis." In "The Precious Jewel," which turns on the tricking of the trickster, the characters play with one another by clever use of language, by understatement and hyperbole.

Although the six narrators of the *Tales* are identified by name in the introduction, they were not individualized in the existing version, as they are, for instance, in Chaucer's *Canterbury Tales.* The sole exception is in "The Double Change" where the teller is obviously one of the women of the group. Otherwise the narrators retain a formal distance from the action of the stories, com - menting occasionally but never otherwise introducing themselves as an element of the story itself. The narrators do, however, give indications of knowing the characters, being in town at the time of the incident, or having had the story by no more than second hand. They certainly are generally familiar with the geography of each tale.

The geography of the *Tales* is one of the strongest elements contributing to the realism of this collection. All of the stories are set in specific cities or towns. Even when a character leaves a town it is always for another specific place. For instance, in "The Sewed-Up Bride" when Gianella del Mangano, the prospective husband, is not around to marry Laura and obtain the dowry, we are told that he has gone to Chianti on business. Similarly, in the same story, when Monna Mechera da Calenzano attempts to collect the dowry with the imposteur posing as Laura's husband, she finds Zanobi just after he returns from a business trip to Riboja.

Some of the stories concentrate even more carefully on the geography of the particular place. In "The Double Change" almost everything that takes place in Florence, takes place in a very specific place — in Santa Croce, near the Ospedali dei Innocenti, in Piazza San Giovanni. "The Sewed-Up Bride" also mentions many specific places in Florence, like the Or San Michele, where Zanobi and Monna Mechera meet. More often in this story, however, the individual location is more generalized, and the very specific designations are used to show the devotedness of Zanobi by listing the names of various churches where his favorite statues or crucifixes are displayed. The effect of all these place names is to give a certain concreteness to the stories and especially to the more bawdy tales in the collection.

Although specific places are carefully mentioned, it is interesting to note that there is no attempt at description. We come across the names of San Marco or the Cintola, but they are abandonned at the mention. The audience was obviously assumed to have all the background to supply the necessary mental pictures. This naming of places is usedto produce comfortable associations in the reader by giving a very accessible point of entry into the story. It is a device that is, interestingly enough, often used in modern fiction, which has even gone one step farther by mentioning consumer products. Three hundred years from now it is unlikely that the word "Coke" will evoke what is does now for us. In the same way, some one familiar with Tuscany will make many of the necessary associations when reading these *Tales,* but these will not be the same as those of some one in sixteenth-century Florence. The full impact of the real - ism is, therefore, somewhat lost on modern audiences, although by comparison with the *Canterbury Tales* of Chaucer we can certainly see how this device was an important element of Firenzuola's work.

A similar realistic effect is achieved by the use of specific names for the characters. Whether introduced as a main character in a story or sometimes only mentioned in passing, almost all of them have complete names, including a family name, such as the Niccolo in both "The Handsome Slave" and "The Two Friends," who is Niccolo degli Albizi, presumably a member of the Florentine family of this name. The specific naming of characters was probably either an attempt to make fun of or to compliment an associate of the author. In Poggio's *Facetia,* the same device is used, and the names there may be those of the members of the group that met at the Curia and told the stories that are collected in this work.

Although Niccolo degli Albizi is mentioned in two stories, these characters have two completely different life stories. In "The Handsome Slave," the shipwrecked Niccolo manages to return to Florence with his mistress from Tunis to enjoy a rich and happy life in Florence, while the Niccolo of "The Two Friends" wastes his fortune and murders both his lover and his rival and is banished from Florence to Apulia, eventually dying near Naples. The one commonality between the two Niccolo's is the devotion of his friend — in "The Handsome Slave," Coppo, and in "The Two Friends," Lapo.

One clearly identifiable character mentioned — Girolamo Firenzuola — who helps to unite the lovers in "The Double Change," is Agnolo's brother, who, under the name of Folchetto, is also one of the storytellers.

Allegorical characters, such as Love, Avarice, Nature and Fortune, occasionally appear, but they are very weak vestiges of earlier devices which were essential plot movers. Only in "The Handsome Slave," the courtly tale in the cycle, is an allegorical figure given more than passing mention. Here Fortune with her wheel controls the turns of Niccolo's fate.

But these *Tales* are really set in the urban, mercantile and secular world of Renaissance Italy, where the controlling influences are not the morality preached by the clergy or the arbitrary forces of allegorical figures. This is a world where men and women compete for money and sex with all the humor and viciousness that the situation requires. Firenzuola's witty style and fast-paced narration have left us with a series of tales that serve as a bridge from the medieval tale to the picaresque novel — the bridge betweeen Chaucer and Cervantes.

-Eileen Gardiner

PREFACE TO THE FIRST EDITION

Firenzuola is more than a pleasing storyteller: he is a masterly writer who adapts a nervous style to the service of a naturally voluptuous imagination, and the pictures of which are of a colouring sparkling with vivacity. He has been praised for his not having adhered to the language such as Dante, Boccaccio, and Petrarch had formed it, and for having enriched his own with a host of picturesque expressions gathered at the fountain head, namely, bor - rowed from the ordinary manner of speaking. We hear at Florence as in Paris more tropes on one market day, than during several hundred Academical sittings. His some - what considerable work comprises a collection of Oriental Apologues entitled: *Discorsi degli Animali; Ragionamenti d'amore;* two *Discourses on Women's Beauty;* two comedies, *La Triunzia* and *I Lucidi;* a translation of the *Golden Ass,* by Apuleius; poetry in which *Capitoli* slightly sketched and a few desultory pieces, appear. One of them, *Expulsion of new characters uselessly introduced into the Tuscan tongue,* is directed against the Trissino, who wanted to add to the alphabet certain parasitic letters, among others the omega. Two of these works at least were formerly turned into French and seem to have been in great vogue; the *Discorsi degli*

Animali were translated for the first time by Gabriel Cottier, under this heading: *Pleasant and jocose discourses of Animals, with a story not less true than funny lately taken place in the city of Florence,* Lyons, 1556, 16mo, and a second time by Pierre de Larivey; they form part of a treatise entitled: *Two Books in Fabulous Philosophy,* Lyons, 1579, 16 mo. Brantôme was ac - quainted with the *Discorsi delle bellezze delle donne,* or with the French translation. *The Golden Ass* presents this striking feature that Firenzuola, in substituting himself for the Lucius of Apuleius, appropriated to himself not only the author's inventions, but also the hero's mishaps which he takes on his own account, and this affords him the opportunity of recounting to us up to the end, a smattering of his own biography and a regular genealogy of his whole family. Paul Louis Courier, a shrewd judge of these matters, highly appreciated this translation owing to its slightly arch savour. "Without reproducing obscure sentences," he says, "the forgotten terms of Fra Jacopone or of Cavalcanti, Firenzuola borrows from the old Tuscan a host of ingenuous and charming expressions, and his version, in which we may say all the flowers of this admirable language are concentrated, is, in many persons' opinion, what is most finished in Italian prose."

The *Ragionamenti d'Amore* commend themselves by the same agreeableness of style and, moreover, the Romances for which they serve as frame are so many short masterpieces of sprightly narrative and ingenious wit. This is evidently his most vivid creation, the one which assures him the greatest chance of being known outside of Italy. Yet they have never before been turned into English, perhaps owing to their title, which does not promise much interest; perhaps because of the too refined insipidness of the preliminaries, which but little lead us to suspect how much boldness and fantasy the author is about to display. In imitation of Boccaccio, Firenzuola sup - poses that a society of young ladies and gallant knights is united in a pleasant villa; they spend the time in prolonged chattings which by their object recall the quintessenced abstractions of the Courts of Love, and, having, about nightfall, chosen a Queen, they relate one after another merry tales in which, by a satirical contrast, the heavenly Venus, so mystically exalted during the preliminaries, is sacrificed without the least hesitation to the earthly Venus. Perhaps this is a symbolical turning adopted by the author to make us comprehend that pure and ideal love, though excellent as a topic of conversation, is no longer current in real life.

However witty this frame may be, it does not possess originality enough to claim much of our attention; we have therefore overlooked the metaphysical discussions at the beginning of the *Ragionamenti* and translated only the Romances which form their conclusion. We shall give a sufficient idea of the whole in stating that the scene is laid at Pozzolatico, near Florence, within the prescribed decorations of this sort of semi-allegorical compositions: terraced gardens, plashing fountains, purling streams, shady groves, meadows decked with flowers, and that the interlocutors are six in number, three gentlemen: Celso, Folchetto, Selvagio, and three ladies: Costanza Amaretta, Fioretta, and Bianca. Celso is Firenzuola himself; he assumes this title in many other works of his; he appears to have designated under the names of Fioretta and Bianca, his sister and sister-in-law; under that of Folchetto, Bianca's husband, his own brother, Girolamo Firenzuola. As to Costanza Amaretta, who is taken as

Queen, she was a Florentine of high descent and great wit whom Firenzuola loved with a tender love, and she died young, in the full splendour of her beauty. He conserved for her a kind of worship and, in his *Epistola in lode delle donne,* addressed to a learned Sienese, Claudio Tolomei, after having placed her for her talents and beauty in the same rank as the most illustrious of whom ancient or modern history makes mention — Sappho, Aspasia, Cornelia, Calpurnia, Sempronia, the Marchioness of Pescara, etc., he compares her for virtues to Plato's Diotima, to Saint Monica, the mother of Saint Augustin. But notwithstanding the aureola of chastity with which he piously surrounds her form, he fails not to let her hear with attentive ears a series of tales the principal features of which would disfigure neither the *Moyen de Parvenir,* nor the *Dames Galantes* of Brantôme.

It has been asked whether it is quite true, as some of the ancient titles have it, that the author of these amusing tales and of the *Capitoli* which are not less so, had ever worn the Benedictine habit. Tiraboschi seriously doubts it, for the convincing reason that if Firenzuola was a monk he would have known how to keep a stricter guard over his imagination. The argument is a queer one: the same as if somebody said that Rabelais must not have been Parish Priest of Meudon, since he wrote *Gargantua* and *Pantagruel.* Firenzuola lived and died a Benedictine. Indeed Canon Moreni discovered in the *Bullarium Archiepiscopale* of Florence a brief of Clement VII, dated 1526, annulling his monastic vows, under the pretext that his taking the habit and his profession were not according to the rules; but another act much later on, passed at Prato in 1539, shows us "the Reverendus Dom Angelus Florentiola, usufructuary and perpetual Administrator of the Abbey of San Salvator of Vaiano, of the order of Vallombrosa," constituting his brother, Girolamo Firenzuola, as procurator of the Convent. He had therefore remained always attached to the order, in spite of this annulling brief, which cannot be explained. Moreover, the *Ragionamenti* are previous to it; Firenzuola, who had nothing printed during his lifetime, dedicated them in 1525 to the Marquis of Camerino, and, still more, he had read the first Day's Work, the only one he achieved, to Clement VII, who expressed himself highly pleased with it. We have in respect to this author's own testimony: "I will and may boast of this, that the judicious ear of Clement the seventh, whose praises no quill however good it be could sufficiently trace, in presence of the greatest minds of Italy, remained wide open several hours listening to the sound of my own voice, while I was reading to him the *Expulsion of Letters* and the first Day's Work of these *Ragionamenti,* which I have just dedicated to the Most Illustrious Signora Caterina Cibo, very honourable Duchess of Camerino."

This remembrance recalled to him the moment of his highest favour in the Pontifical Court. Let us give a few facts of his biography. He was born at Florence in 1493, of a family from Firenzuola, a small town at the foot of the Alps, between Florence and Bologna, whence its ascendants have taken the name. His great-grandfather and grandfather filled important offices in the house of the Medicis; his father, Sebastiano Firenzuola, being successively judge and public notary, discharged the functions of Chancellor, appointed by election as overseer of the city magistrates. His mother was the daughter of Alesandro Braccasi, an estimable scholar, the author of a good translation of Appian, and he was moreover first

secretary of the Republic under the grand Dukes
Lawrence and Peter de Medicis; he died at Rome, as
ambassador of Florence with Alexander VI; Firenzuola
got a mausoleum erected to him within the basilic of the
Convent of Saint Praxedes, of which he was an abbot.
Destined by his family to the ecclesiastical state, he went
to study canon law at Siena, then at Perugia, where he
became acquainted with the famous Pietro Aretino and
formed lasting relations with him. These studies shocked
him; he complains somewhere of being consumed in them
with great pains and without any pleasure the best part of
his youth. He attained nevertheless to a doctor's degree
and at once betook himself, about the year 1516, to Rome,
where he was attached to the Curia. Under the pontificate
of Clement VII, several documents being found by his
biographers mark him out as entrusted with the defence
of a certain number of cases, in the capacity of procura -
tor, and invested at the same time with the titles of abbot
of Saint Praxedes and Saint Mary the Hermit, of Spoleto.
Although he had nothing printed, his manuscript works
were sufficiently scattered about to win him a lawful
renown.   He was besides a man of jovial humour,
esteemed for the amenity of his character.   "You will
diffuse mirth into the souls of those who familiarly
frequent you," writes to him the divine Aretino.
'Remember how I knew you as a schoolboy at Perugia, as
a citizen at Florence, as a prelate in Rome." In another
letter he reminds him of his kind turns with the Pope. "I
still have a recollection," says he, "of the great pleasure
with which Pope Clement felt, the evening I prevailed on
him to read what you had just composed on the *Omegas* of
the Trissino. It was this that determined His Holiness, at
the same time as Monsignor Bembo, to be eager to know

you in person." We have seen further back Firenzuola reading to the Pope not only his witty diatribe against the Trissino, but also the first Day's Work of the *Ragionamenti;* the Popes of that time listened to wonton tales, assisted at representations of Machiavel's *Mandragola,* or Cardinal Bibbiena's *Calandra,* and laughed as simple mortals.

The death of Clement VII, in 1534, the disgust which Firenzuola felt for his juridical functions and especially a pernicious fever, the famous fever of the Pontine Marshes, which sometimes renders a stay in Rome very dangerous, obliged him to abandon the curia. He obtained the Abbey of Vaiano, near Cremona, but tarried especially either at Florence or Prato, and endeavoured to establish in a more wholesome air his ruined health. The fever was a long while about yielding up; it worked upon him during seven whole years, after having worn him out to a skeleton:

"I had become of so livid a hue that I looked like a Sienese, returned not many weeks hence from the Maremma. Ah! wretched man! had I fallen asleep at church among the Monks, they would have taken me in the very midst of my nap for one dead, and buried me. Och! the money I spent to get well! I would have been better had I lost it at cards, for in the end it was all one to me. I absorbed a whole grocery ware, and had more clysters administered to me than the Bishop of Scala, when he was in the world. I think I broke two hundred chamber pots, first at Rome, next at Florence, and wore out the greatest physicians."

In fine, he got rid of it thanks only to a decoction of guaiacum, the "holy wood" so famous in the sixteenth century for its curative virtues; Firenzuola being *lode del legno santo,* to which the preceeding quotation belongs. Yet his death came on in 1544 or 1545, having closely followed the establishment of his health; he had at least, like that patient of whom a wag of a doctor spoke, the consolation of dying cured. He had the impudence of returning to Rome, and he was buried near his father, within the church of his ancient Abbey of Saint Praxedes.

This long sickness is perhaps the reason why the *Ragionamenti d'amore,* his chief work, remained unfinished. They were published, such as they were, with a few others of his works, by his brother Girolamo, under the following head: *Prose di M. Agnolo Firenzuola, Fiorentino; in Fiorenza, appresso Lorenzo Torrentino, impressor ducale,* 1552. Firenzuola intended to add five more arranged after the same plan, to the first Day's Work, composed of preliminary conversations and six romances. Later on they found in his papers four more romances, matter prepared beforehand for one of the subsequent Day's Work. In this translation they come under the numbers V, VI, VII, and VIII. We give the whole ten in the order adopted by the former editors, who modified Firenzuola's arrangement in order to make the ten recitals fit into the frame of but one Day's Work. Such as they are, these tales give pleasure by their free allure, their jovial tone, and the perfect finish of their style, far more than by the idle dissertations and chattings which serve them as transitions or entries into the matter; they cause us to deeply regret that the author has not written more of them.

* *

*

I

THE HANDSOME SLAVE

Long ago there lived in this COUNTRY TWO YOUNG MEN OF HIGH DESCENT, WELL BLESSED WITH THE GIFTS OF FORTUNE. THEY WERE NOT CONTENT WITH THE VALIANT EXPLOITS OF their ancestors and did not consider the action of others as genuine illustrations, so they rendered themselves famous and praiseworthy on their own to give more splendor to their nobility than they received from it. By their culti-vated minds, their courtesy and the thousand occupations in which they were engaged, they acquired so high a renown in Florence that whoever could speak most in praise of them was indeed considered happy. What was especially praiseworthy in them was a certain tender friendship, a brotherly love that united them so that when one went anywhere, the other went with him, and the desire of one of them was the desire of the other.

While these two men were thus living an honorable and quiet life, Fortune had, you might say, begrudged them it. For it turned out that one of the two, Niccolo degli Albizi, received news of the death of one of his uncles on his mother's side, a rich merchant of Valencia, who, without son or nearer kin, had appointed Niccolo his sole heir. It was then his duty, since he wanted to see to his own affairs in person, to make up his mind about going to Spain, and he invited Coppo, his friend, to ac - company him; an invitation that was most welcome. They had already fixed the day and way of traveling, when their misfortune — or doubtless their good luck — would have it that Coppo's father, Giambattista Canigiani, was stricken just at the time of starting by so frightful a sick - ness that he departed from this life for the next in a couple of hours. Now, if Niccolo wanted to set out, he had to go alone. He said goodbye to his friend most reluctantly, es - pecially under such trials, but, forced by sheer necessity, he set out toward Genoa and, having taken a berth on a Genoese vessel, had the anchor weighed at once.

Fortune was most averse to his voyage. He had not yet gone more than a hundred miles from land when about sunset the sea, becoming all at once foam, began to rise and threaten by a thousand signs imminent danger to the passengers. The captain, wishing to take his precautions, accordingly prepared for it in the greatest hurry, but the rain and wind came on suddenly with so much violence that nothing of what was necessary could be done. Again the night fell in an instant so pitch dark that they could no longer distinguish any object on earth, save when a flash of lightening occasionally broke to make the situation still more horrible and dreadful, then plunged everything anew into darkness. What a pity to behold those poor passengers so often doing precisely what they should not, while they were also trying to meet the threats of heaven! If the captain gave any commands, nobody heard him, because the rain was falling in torrents, the roaring billows were dashing against one another, the cordage was straining, the sails flapping, the lightning flashing and the thunder roaring. The greater the necessity, the greater need they had of common sense and courage. What courage could these poor creatures have, in your opinion, on now seeing the ship apparently attempting to jump up to the sky, then cleaving the billows as if intending to fling herself into hell? Do you think their hair stood on end when it looked as if the firmament, having turned into water, wanted to drop into the sea; then the sea swelling wanted to fly to the assault? What hope do you think they had when they saw that the others cast into the deep what they held most precious, when they flung their wealth into it to avoid a worse destiny for themselves?

The vessel dislocated and abandoned to the mercy of the winds, now tossed about by them, now shattered by the waves, all filled with water, was going in search of some rock to put an end to the toils of the unhappy seamen, who, not knowing what else to do, threw them - selves into one another's arms, embraced, sobbed and cried for mercy with all their might. Oh! How many among them would have liked to console the others, who were themselves in need of consolation and whose voices were smothered with sighs and tears! Oh! How many among them, but a little while before, defied heaven and now seemed like nuns at prayer! Who implored the Virgin Mary, who Saint Nicholas of Bari, who yelled after Saint Elmo, who talked of going to the Holy Sepulcher, who of turning monk and who of taking a wife for God's sake? One merchant swears to make resti - tution, another to cease usury, one calls on his father, another his mother; this one remembers his friends, another his children. What rendered the common cala -

mity a thousand times more horrible was to see the misery of one taking pity on another, to hear all these bewailings.

While the unhappy creatures were in this painful situation, the topmast was broken by a sudden sally of the tempest, and the vessel was smashed into a thousand pieces, sending most of the passengers into the dreaded deep, there to fill the maws of fish and other marine beasts. The rest, more skillful or less ill-used by Fortune, provided for their safety by holding onto planks. Niccolo had, among the latter, grasped a plank, which he only let go of when it landed him on the coast of Barbary, near Sousa, a few miles from Tunis.

Cast up here and discovered by some fishermen who had come to fish, his condition moved them to pity. They picked him up and carried him off to a shelter nearby, where they lit a fire and placed him close to it. After they had taken great pains and restored him to his senses, they got him to talk. They noticed he spoke Latin, from which they correctly assumed that he must be a Christian and without further thought of catching a better fish that morning they unanimously agreed to take him to Tunis, where they sold him as a slave to a powerful country gentleman named Hajji Akhmet.

This man, seeing that the newcomer was young and goodlooking, thought of keeping him in his own service, and Niccolo showed so many proofs of cleverness and diligence in his duties that he endeared himself in a very short time to his master and to the whole household.

He became especially a favorite with Akhmet's wife, one of the most courteous, gentle and comely women that had ever been or were still on those shores. He pleased her so well that she was no longer happy day or night except when she saw him or heard him speaking; and she knew so nicely how to get around her husband, who would have imagined anything else but what was really her object, that he made her a present of Niccolo, so that she might keep him in her own service. The lady was most highly delighted at this, and she curbed her amorous flames for a long while.

Her intention at first was to feed them in secret, without Niccolo's knowing anything about it; but from being constantly in his company they grew so trouble - some that she was forced to satisfy them one way or another, and she had more than once the intention of disclosing her passion to him. Now, every time she was about to put her project into execution, the shame of being in love with a slave, the dread of not being able to rely on him, the great dangers to which she was exposing her honor and her life, suddenly baffled her.

Retiring frequently alone, fired in different senses, she used to say to herself, "Extinguish then this flame, while it is only just beginning to kindle. At present a little water will do, but later on, if it gains ground over me all the water in the sea will not suffice. Ah! Blind woman that you are, do you not consider the infamy you will heap on yourself if ever anyone comes to know that you have bestowed your love on a stranger, a slave, a Christian? You will no sooner have let him see one glimpse of liberty that he will profit by the occasion to fly away and abandon you. Oh miserable one to bewail your folly! Don't you know that while thought is wandering, love can have nothing stable? Withdraw from this nonsensical under - taking, let your foolish love vanish, and if you will at any price stain your honesty, let it be in favor of someone who will not afterwards be a matter of shame to you, so that you may excuse yourself in the eyes of those who may have heard of your imprudence.

"But to whom am I speaking, O unfortunate one? To whom am I addressing such supplications? How can I have a will of my own, I who belong to another? These thoughts, these projects, these delibertaions, do not become you, O wedded wife. They are for those who can dispose of themselves as they please. They do not become one who is in the power of a man as I am. I must turn my ear to the side where the voice of the master calls me. Turn then, O foolish one, turn your words to better use, lose time no longer, waste yourself away no more. What you will not do today, you will be forced to do tomorrow while running the greatest risks.

"See if your lover's will becomes one and the same with your own, and know that, stranger as he is, he ought not to be held the less estimable for that, either by you or by anyone else. If we were to set a high price only on the productions of your own country, I cannot see why gold, pearls and other precious objects should be of so great value, as they really are outside countries that produce them. Fortune has made a slave of him, but she has not on that account robbed him of his pleasant manners, nor does it prevent me from recognizing the greatness of his soul or from beholding the splendor of his merits. Fortune alters nothing at birth. It may happen to anyone to become a slave. It is not his fault. It is Fortune's. There - fore, I ought to despise Fortune and not him. And if it had happened to me to become a slave, it would not make me in the bottom of my soul other than I am. Then let these motives not prevent me from wishing him well.

"Is it because he belongs to another religion that I should be the more averse to him? Well, what of that, O

foolish one? Am I more certain of my religion than of
his? Supposing I had a thousand times all the certainty in
the world about it. I do not deny it on that account, I do
not the slightest thing contrary to our gods. Yet who
knows if, loving and beloved by him, I shall not prevail
over him to believe in our law? I shall thus perform an
act at once agreeable to myself and our gods.

"Why struggle against myself and be an enemy to my
own pleasures? Why not obey my own inclinations? Did
I fancy myself able to resist the laws of love? What inno -
cence of soul were mine if I, who am but a poor silly
woman, the frail target of Cupid's darts, should think
myself able to keep my guard against what thousands of
the wisest men could not escape! Let my passion then
triumph over every other consideration. Let the feeble
force of a tender young woman no longer try to struggle
against that of so powerful a master!"

After the enamored woman reasoned and fought with
herself many times, she finally, thanks to her own good
will, granted victory to the side toward which Love had
urged her. No sooner had she imagined an opportunity
when she drew Niccolo aside and told him of her torments
and pleaded for his love. Niccolo was quite bewildered at
first on hearing of this, and all sorts of fancies whirled
through his brain. He was afraid that she acted this way
only to put him to the test, and he had half a mind to make
her a threatening answer. But remembering certain kind -
nesses she used to grant him and considering her more
discrete than the women of that country generally, he
thought of the romance of the Count of Antwerp and the
Queen of France, and a thousand other similar situations,
and he considered the occasion favorable, whatever
should become of it, to reply that he was wholly disposed

to obey her wishes, which he did. Nevertheless, whether he wanted to give the affair a greater relish or whether he wished to try himself or for whatever reason, he kept her many days in suspense before deciding on it.

When she, who desired more than empty words, clapped the saddle on his back, as the saying goes, he, who saw by a thousand signs that he was her master, resolved to make her a Christian to further his own ends before satisfying her. With fair and well-prepared words he told her how he was at her command, but he entreated her beforehand to promise that she would do a very simple thing, which he would ask of her. The woman, on whom time weighed like a thousand years until the final putting of the business into operation, without thinking what he could want, and out of her wits through such ardent desire, pledged him her faith and swore a thousand oaths to do whatever he should request. At that Niccolo gently explained to her the nature of his resolution.

At first the imposed condition seemed very hard to the poor creature, and were it not, as she incessantly re - peated, that she was ever doomed to follow the will of another, I do not doubt that she would have refused to commit this folly. But Love, who is so well accustomed to perform miracles, knew too how to persuade her so that after many hesitations and excuses she was forced to say, "Do with me as you please." So, to cut a long story short, on the same day she received baptism and these two were betrothed, and on the same day they consummated their marriage, and the mysteries of this new religion seemed so sweet to her that, after the example of Alibech, she constantly upbraided herself for having delayed so long in trying it. She loved so well to be within its embrace and thoroughly instructed therein, that she no longer had any happiness except when inculcating herself on some new doctrine.

While Niccolo was teaching and she learning, and while they were both at so mild a school, without anybody getting the slightest clue to the secret, Niccolo's friend, Coppo, received news of Niccolo's adventure and, thoroughly resolved to ransom his friend, came with a large sum of money to the coast of Barbary. He arrived at Tunis and hardly had he landed when he met Niccolo, who was by chance returning from somewhere with his mistress. After they recognized one another, not without difficulty, they embraced and kissed at least a thousand times. The moment he learned of his friend's purpose, Niccolo offered him suitable thanks, forbade him to hint a word about his ransom until they talked it over again, for a reason that he would explain to him later. He then pointed out a place where they could see each other the next day and, without further discourse, left him.

The wife wanted to know at once who that man was and what conversation they had together, for she was torn by jealousy, fearing not only that any person whatever, but even the bird flitting through space, might carry off her dear lover. He managed to satisfy her by means of a few stories of his own making.

Niccolo had, as anyone may imagine, a very great desire to return home. Knowing for certain, however, that if his passionate young wife discovered anything about it, she would utterly ruin him or at least undermine his projects, he wavered at attempting the slightest thing at all. This was why he did not wish Coppo to hint a word about it to anybody. For my part I think that this love would have placed before his eyes so many perils and obstacles that he would have resigned himself to stay where Fortune had cast him, for love was deeply rooted within his heart from long habit and, as you know, *"Love dispenses no man beloved from loving."*

He had sense enough to see that this woman was allowing herself to be carried away by her passion for him, and that Hajji Akhmet would at last find out their secret. For this reason he more than once thought of seeing whether she would be willing to go to his country. He saw her so blinded for his sake that he felt sure that he would not have much trouble in persuading her, but since he had not yet resolved the problem of ways and means he remained silent up to this moment.

Now that Coppo was here, and thinking that his coming was opportune and that the plan would now succeed far more easily, he thought it necessary to talk to his friend before dealing with the ransom. Having then found Coppo and having thoroughly treated all of the pros and cons of the case, they finally agreed upon what was to be done if the woman consented.

Niccolo chose a favorable time and place and after greeting her he said, "My very dear mistress, to think of what one would have done when another has fallen into a misfortune that he might have avoided, is nothing else than to wish, without knowing anything about it, to show oneself wise after the accident. It therefore appears to me necessary, if we do not wish to be numbered among such people, to avoid the dangerous defiles into which our love is leading us before we break our necks. Love has ren - dered us so reckless that, as you may judge still better than I, if we do not remedy it, I feel that it will be the cause of our downfall. This is why I have thought to myself more than once of a way that we can escape from such a danger. Out of a certain number that I have considered I can think of two that are easier than the rest. The first is that we should decide to gradually end our loving relationship. If your ardor is equal to mine that way will seem so hard that any other course, no matter how difficult, will be less painful by comparison. So, in my mind, the second has always pleased me more, although it must seem to you at first very burdensome and difficult to carry out. I do not doubt, though, that after thinking it over well, you will finish by finding it smiling invitingly upon you to decide and choose it boldly. You shall see your lover's, your husband's, interest and honor springing from it, and you shall see the opportunity for enjoying our love forever without anguish of soul and without peril.

"My plan is for you to go with me to our lovely Italy. What a country it is compared to this, we will leave for future discussion. Besides, you have often heard it spoken of both by me and by others. Florence, the pleasant place of my birth, is situated in the center. It has the mildest climate and it is — be it said without disparaging others — surely the finest city in the whole world. I will not speak of churches, palaces, private dwellings, streets straight as gun barrels, fine and spacious squares, all that is within the walls; why, the outskirts, the gardens, the villas with which it is more copiously supplied than any other city, these will appear to you as so many paradises, and should God grant us the grace of arriving there safely, he knows how happy you will live there and how you will upbraid yourself for not having been the first to request it.

"But let us lay aside what may be advantageous and pleasing to you. I know that you set but little value on that compared with what is advantageous and pleasing to me. Even though everything should avert you from this resolution, would it not suffice, in order to persuade you, to think of the wretched state out of which you would take your lover, your spouse? He loves you so fervently that he prefers to live a bondsman in a foreign land, when he could have freedom in his own, rather than abandon you. Yes," he said, "for henceforth the means for redeeming me are not wanting, provided that the love I bear you permits me to do as I like with myself.

"That Christian to whom I was speaking the other day has almost come to an understanding with your husband, but please God, I shall not leave without my lady, my mistress, my soul! I know her love for me is so strong, her confidence in my words so unbounded that it seems to me I behold her already fix her thoughts on this means which to my mind is the most propitious.

"Why do you hesitate? What is holding you, Signora, that I hear you not pronounce, as promptly as I could have wished, some loving word? Perhaps it seems impossible to leave your fatherland? If I am your happiness, as you have a thousand times declared, where I shall be, will you not have your country, your spouse, your all?

"The more you leave behind you here, the more you shall find over there, even a hundredfold, and you will be so delighted in frequenting our ladies, especially one of my little sisters, that you will think you have left the wild forests to come and live among human beings. This sister of mine will love and cherish you dearly when she learns of your kindness to me, and you will surely bless the day when you arrived in that delightful country. This is not the time to discuss the merits of other men with you; besides you have solved the question yourself long ago. Yet if I have pleased and still please you to such a degree that you bestow on me your own sweet self, I, who look more like a countryman than a brave champion, the more then will the other men be pleasing to you, for they have more graces than I.

"What keeps you, now that all other reasons counsel you to fly? Would it be the dread of what might be said of you in this country after your departure? Ah, Signora, do not let that either hinder you from doing what is so advantageous to us both. Not that honor ought not to be placed above all, and I confess the opinion is good of those who claim that we must not mind the evil that people say of us so long as their words do not reach our ears. But neither you nor anybody else ought to be troubled about a reproach wrongfully aimed, as it would be in your case should anyone reprove you in this. Who can backbite you with righteous teeth to embrace the true one, because you have fled far from those who are deadly enemies to us Christians? Who will blame you for having entered the land of your spouse, for having dragged him out of slavery? Nobody of sound judgment. On the contrary, there will be a host of persons to congratulate you, to extol you to the skies.

"Of what are you thinking then, my darling soul? What is keeping you back? Would it be, forsooth, the hardship and peril, which you know are inseparable from the enterprise? If that is so, I can assure you there would be little risk; whereas to remain here, to conduct our - selves as our mutual love compels us, is obviously dangerous. Now, who is there who would not expose himself to an uncertain peril in order to avoid another that he knows to be most certain? As to the difficulties, I shall take charge of them myself; and I so swear to you upon my faith, if God does not deprive me of your favor, which enables me to live happy even in bondage. I have found through that friend, with whom you so often find me in conversation, the means of our getting away in all safety on one of his vessels. Consider, my darling mistress, what confidence I have in you that I should disclose to you such grave projects. Reflect on all the good things that we stand to gain, and give no thought to the dangers and difficulties. Get ready then to free me from bondage, get ready to take me to my beloved city, to your city, to my sister who, with tearful and outstretched arms, implores you to restore me to her, and who offers you a loving welcome." He accompanied these last words with deep-drawn sighs, which would have moved eternal hills. Then he went silent.

Niccolo's words so deeply touched the heart of the tender young woman that, although it appeared to her cruel and preposterous to take such a resolution, although she felt a thousand difficulties, a thousand perils pass through her head, she was thinking at the same time of all those perfidies, which, they say, men practice toward women silly enough to love you. Urged on by her great love, which smoothed down for her all the mountains, she, like the courageous woman she was, told him without more ado, that she was ready to do his will.

To cut a long story short, after he had arranged with Coppo the when and the how and had procured the necessary supplies, the woman, having previously made provision of a fair share of gold and silver and other valuables, pretended one fine morning to go out for a walk and went with Niccolo to the coast where Coppo's ship was moored. The moment they arrived, she and all those who were to cross over pretended they wanted to visit the ship and, leaving the others on shore, embarked and speedily gave the sails to the wind, and before the bystanders were aware of what had happened, the ship was a mile from the shore.

When they realized the trick that had been played on them they were amazed and angered and they straightway informed Hajji Akhmet. You can imagine what a fuss was made and how everything was done to overtake them, but the wind was so favorable that they had almost reached Sicily before the pursuit began. They landed at Messina because the lady, being but sadly accustomed to so many fatigues, was in need of rest. They therefore made up their minds to go into the heart of the town and put up at the best hotel they could find, which they did.

Now it happened that the court was transferred to Messina during those days, and an ambassador of the king of Tunis having come with the king of Sicily to handle some very weighty affairs, was staying at the same hotel as our heros, as ill-luck would have it. He noticed, I know not how often, the young woman secretly, so to speak, fancied he knew her and, while thus remaining in doubt, there arrived from his prince some letters informing him about her flight and ordering him, if she happened to land in that country, to use all his endeavors with the king and whomever he needed to have her brought back to her husband. As soon as he had perused the letters, the ambassador knew for certain that this was she, and he went immediately to the king and unfolded to him his prince's commands.

Without any delay the king summoned the woman and the two young men before him. He had no trouble in per - ceiving that it was she whom they were looking for and, desiring to do something pleasing to the king of Tunis, commanded that they should be sent back at once without any argument.

What grief for the poor young woman, for her unhappy Niccolo and for Coppa too when they heard such sorrowful news! Oh! what cries, what tears and what prayers! I should never have the heart to tell one thou - sandth of them. Taken back by force to the harbor and reembarked on the same ship, the command of which the king had confided to a man on whom he relied, they were brought back to Barbary as prisoners of the king of Tunis.

Thanks to more favorable weather than they would have desired, they had already gotten within a few miles of the creek of Carthagena, when Fortune, tired at last of so many annoyances and toils conjured up against poor Niccolo, resolved to give the wheel a turn. She caused so terrible a wind and tempest to rage that the ship was driven violently back and, within a few hours — the thing is scarcely believable — she was carried out into the Tyrrhenian Sea off Livorno. Despoiled of her mast and rigging and quite disabled, she fell into the hands of Pisan corsairs who allowed the young lady and two young men to redeem themselves for a large sum of money.

The three took themselves to Pisa. They stayed there some time to establish the young lady's health, which was troubled by so many fatigues and chagrins. When she looked sufficiently recovered, they set out for Florence. The kind reception, the festivities, the caresses with which they were loaded on their return, I could not imagine, much less describe.

After the young woman had lived a few days in joy, when she had become as strong and gay as Niccolo desired, he had her baptized and christened Beatrix. The town made a general holiday of the event.

II

THE METAMORPHOSIS

A T TIVOLI, AN ANCIENT CITY OF
THE LATINS, THERE WAS A GENTLEMAN NAMED
CECC' ANTONIO FORNARI, WHO HAD THE IDEA OF
TAKING A WIFE AT AN AGE WHEN OTHER MEN HAVE A
thousand griefs from theirs, and, as is the case with old
men, he would not take one unless she was young and
good-looking. He lit on the right thing.

One of the Coronati, named Giusto, and a man of some
note be it said, seeing himself overstocked with a batch of
daughters and so as not to be obliged to hand out a large
dowry, gave the old man one of them, a pretty and comely
lass. She, on seeing herself tied up to an old fellow fallen
back into childhood and from now on deprived of those
pleasures for which she had long wished to abandon her
home and parents, became very angry about it. She soon
grew so disgusted at the spitting, wheezing and other
trophies of her husband's old age, that she thought of
making herself amends and got it into her head to take on,
should the occasion present itself, somebody who could
supply the wants of her youth better than her father had
known how to do.

19

Fortune was more favorable to her schemes than she had dared to hope. In fact, a young Roman named Fulvio Macaro, made his way to Tivoli with his friend Menico Coscia for some diversion. He frequently glimpsed the young woman who appeared to him pretty, as indeed she was, and fell ardently in love with her. Entrusting this Menico with the secret of his love, he commended himself to him for his help.

Menico, who was a man to get out of any scrape, told his friend to be of good cheer and that if he was resolved on following out his idea in everything, he well knew how to settle matters in a way that would enable him to be with the young woman as often as he liked. You can imagine how Fulvio, who had no other desire, then told him to call on him the next day, but Menico replied that he was prepared to go into the matter at once, provided his friend helped. "I have been told," said Menico, "that the lady's husband is on the lookout for a slip of a girl about fifteen for housework, and he will marry her off at the end of a few years, as is still the custom in Rome. I have deter - mined that it shall be you who will go to him, to remain there as long as you please, but listen a while how. Our neighbor, that man from Tagliacozzo who comes some - times to our place to do one thing or another is, as you know, a great friend of mine. While talking to me yester - day about one thing or another, he told me that the old fellow had commissioned him to procure the servant, and to do this he was going home in a few days to see if he could find anyone there. He is poor and willingly offers his services to the rich. I feel sure that for a small gift he would do whatever we wish. Let him then pretend that he has gone to Tagliacozzo and is to return thence in a fortnight or so. He will dress you up like a village girl and, passing you off for one of his relations, will place you in the lady's mansion. Once there you will only have yourself to blame if your courage fails you. What will help you in all this is the whiteness of your skin, your beardlesness and the fact that you have a womanish face, which has often made people think you were a woman dressed up as a man. Besides, as your nurse belonged to that village, I think you will be able to talk like a native." The poor lover agreed to all this, and it seemed to him that he must wait an eternity for the scheme to be put into execution. In his imagination he was already with the lady helping her with the housework.

Without wasting a single moment the two friends hurried off to find the countryman, who was very glad with the commission; and they settled beforehand every - thing that was to be done.

Before a month had gone by Fulvio was working as a housemaid to the lady, who was named Lavinia, so dili - gently that not only she but the whole household had the warmest regard for him. While remaining in this posi - tion, Lucia — as he called himself — was waiting for an opportunity of being serviceable to her other than in making the bed, and it happened that Cecc' Antonio went to spend a few days in Rome, and Lavinia, seeing herself left alone, had the whim of taking Lucia to sleep with her.

On the first night after they got between the sheets (to one of them, all mirthful at the unexpected windfall, it seemed a thousand years until the other fell asleep to gather while she slept the fruit of her turmoils) the other thinking of some young blade who was shaking the dust off her fur better than her husband, began to embrace and kiss Lucia most affectionately and, as may happen, her hand just strayed toward the side where one distinguishes a boy from a girl. Finding she was not a woman like her - self there, she greatly wondered and drew her hand back, not less astounded than she would have been if she sudden - ly had felt a snake under a tuft of grass.

Lucia, not daring to say or do anything to affect the outcome of the scheme, and Lavinia, doubting that this was the servant, stared aghast; yet, seeing that it was indeed Lucia but not venturing to speak to her, she thought of putting her hand again on the object of her astonishment, found it the same as at first, and felt un - certain as to whether she were awake or dreaming. Then thinking that perhaps her touch might be deceiving her, she lifted the clothes, wishing to assure herself with her own eyes. She not only beheld with her eyes what she had touched with her hands, but discovered a heap of snow having the form of a man and the tint of fresh roses, so that she was compelled to admit the evidence and to believe that so great a change was miraculously wrought that she might safely taste the sweetness of love during the days of her youth.

Being quite encouraged she turned toward Lucia and said, "Oh what do I see there this night with my own doubting eyes? I know right well that you were now just a girl and lo, you are now become a boy. How is that? I fear I see awry or that instead of Lucia you are some evil spirit come to my bed to make me fall into wicked temptations. Indeed I must see to the bottom of this." While saying this she slipped under Lucia and began to excite the spot with those provocations that frolicsome girls willingly use on precocious young brats. With this game she assured herself that it was not a spirit bewitched and that she had not seen amiss, and she had such comfort from this as you yourself may imagine.

But do not think that she considered herself out of doubt the first time or even the third. Such mysteries are not to be accepted lightly, and I can assure you that if she had not feared for the changing of the real Lucia into a ghost, she would have believed herself quite certain of the fact only after the sixth test.

When this stage had been reached she passed from deeds to words and tenderly enquired by what manner of means the change had come about. So Lucia, recalling the events since the first day of her love, related the whole story to her. Lavinia was exceedingly glad to see herself loved by so pretty a youth and to know how he had ex - posed himself to many turmoils and perils for her sake. Passing from this account to other moving discourses, and perhaps still wishing to come to a certainty for a seventh time, they tarried so long that the sun was already peeping through the window. The moment to get up seemed to have arrived, and after deciding that Lucia should remain a girl during the daytime for everybody and become a boy at night or whenever they might find a way to be alone, they left the room all joyful.

This happy accord lasted a long while. Months passed without anyone in the house becoming aware of anything, and it would have continued so for years had not Cecc' Antonio — although he was, as I have said, altogether beyond the age and his donkey could hardly carry the corn to the mill once a month — seeing Lucia tripping about the house and considering her pretty good-looking, thought about discharging a sieveful into her press and teased her several times with his urgent entreaties. Lucia, fearing that some scandal might result from it one fine day, pleaded to Lavinia for God's sake to rid her of such an annoyance.

I have no need to tell you whether the gnat pricked her or whether she hummed a blindman's litany the first time she had an interview with her husband. All I can certify is that she called him something less than lord. "Look at the bold foot-soldier who wants to go through the drills like a cavalier! Well I never! What would you be like if you were young and jolly? You who no longer have to occupy yourself with anything except with the graveyard and await every moment the final decree! A pretty smack in the face you want to give me! Leave, you old fool, leave sin as it has left you. Do you not know that even if you were steel, you would not be capable of forming the tip of a Damascus needle? Oh it would do you great honor when you would have reduced this poor girl, who is as good as bread, to what I will not name! That will be her dowry to serve for a husband. How pleased her parents will be! How merry all her relations will be when they discover they have entrusted their ewe lamb to the care of wolves! Tell me briefly, nasty man, if that was done to you, what would you think about it? What! have you not set all Paradise in a stir these latter days because I was serenaded? But do you know what I have to tell you? You will make me think of things of which I never dreamt up to now; oh yes! oh yes! you shall have something to make you merry one of these fine days. Just you wait a bit; I shall put in your way what you are looking for, and since I understand that by conducting myself well it suc - ceeds but ill with me, I shall now try if conducting myself badly does not succeed better. Whoever will have fair weather in this low deceitful world, has only to do evil!" As she accompanied these last words with four wicked lit - tle tears forcibly shed, she affected the old scamp so much that he begged her pardon and promised never to rebuke her again. But his promises were of little value. If the tears were feigned, so was the relenting they provoked.

A few days later, Lavinia went to a wedding party, which the people of Tobaldo were celebrating, and left behind Lucia who felt somewhat indisposed. The enter - prising fellow found her lying asleep. Here was his chance! He slipped his hands underneath her skirts and, lifting them to indulge his little pleasure, he lighted on what he little expected. Bewildered, he stood for some time like a lifeless thing; then, revolving a thousand bad thoughts in his head, he began to ask himself what this meant. Lucia had her explanations and excuses quite pat, for long ago she had conferred with Lavinia in case such a thing should crop up. Knowing that he was a jolly old fel - low to believe a fib just as well as the truth and that he was not as terrible in reality as he appeared in words, she did not in the least trouble herself and pretended to be shed - ding bitter tears and implored him to hear her reasons.

After he encouraged her with a few kind words, she began, with trembling voice and downcast eyes, to tell her tale. "Know, my dear lord, that when I came into this house, cursed be the hour I put my foot here since so silly an adventure was to befall me in it, I was not what I am now. Three months ago — my God, sad life is mine! — that thing there came to me. One day as I was washing with lye, I felt a heavy weariness creep over me, and this began to grow so small, so small, then it gradually began increasing in size so thoroughly that it has arrived at the degree you see, and if I had not seen your nephew, the tallest of them, having one like it, I should have thought it was some evil growth, for it sometimes gives me so much trouble that I would prefer to have I know not what. I am so ashamed of it. Yes, indeed, I am so ashamed of it that I have never dared open my mouth about it to anybody. Thus since there is on my part neither fault nor sin, I beseech you for the sake of God and our Good Lady of Olives, to have pity on me. I promise you that I would rather die than that people should learn so shameful a thing about a poor girl such as I."

The dear old man, who was quite out of his depth, seeing the tears raining down her cheeks, and hearing her reciting her reasons so nicely, began almost to believe that she was speaking the truth. Nevertheless, as this change seemed almost too much of a good thing, and recalling the caresses that Lavinia would lavish on Lucia, he suspected some underhanded work and asked himself if Lavinia had not, after finding the thing out, taken advantage of the windfall right under his nose. So he questioned Lucia more explicitly and asked whether her mistress knew about it. "The Lord preserve me!" she boldly replied, seeing that the affair was progressing favorably. "I have always been on my guard against that. I have told you and I repeat it, I would rather die than anyone in the world should know it. If God cures me of this evil, no man except yourself shall know of it; and may God grant, since he brought this infirmity on me, that I may return to my former state! To tell you the truth, I am so grieved about it that I am sure to die soon; for besides the shame it will cause me every time I see you, knowing that you know my story, it seems to me I am the most encumbered creature in the world with this thing — excuse my mentioning it — swinging between my legs."

"Come, my child," replied the old graybeard quite affected, "remain as you are, and say nothing to anybody; perhaps we may find some medicine to cure you; leave it to me, and on no account say a word to your mistress."

Thus, without another word, his head in a whirl, he left her and sought out the local doctor, whom they called Master Consolo, and goodness knows how many more people to enquire about the accident.

Meanwhile Lavinia returned home, and when she learned from Lucia what had happened, I leave you to imagine what she felt. I reckon it was sadder news for her than when she knew she had so old a husband. Cecc' Antonio, who had gone, as I have just stated, to enquire about the malady, having heard so much about it in one way or another, returned home more perplexed than ever. Without saying a word to anybody that night he resolved to set out for Rome the next morning in search of some learned man who knew better how to expound the enigma to him.

At dawn he mounted on his horse and proceeded on his way. He alighted at a friend's house, and after a light repast he repaired to the university, thinking to find there better than elsewhere somebody who would know how to get this fly out of his ear, and by a happy chance he fell precisely on that dear comrade who had got Lucia placed in his household. The young man came sometimes into these quarters for pastime. Our friend, seeing him smart - ly dressed and saluted by a crowd of people, thought that he must be some great scholar, so he led him aside and, under an oath of secrecy, entrusted him with his torment.

Menico, who thoroughly knew the fine old fellow, and who guessed at once how things stood, said to himself while laughing up his sleeve, "You have put up at the right inn, old pal." After a long conversation, he gave him to understand once and for all that the thing was not impossible, but that it had already happened several times.

In order more easily to win his belief, he took him to a bookshop and asked for a Pliny in Italian. He showed him what this author says about a similar case, Book VII, Chapter IV. He then showed him what Battisto Fulgoso writes in his chapter "On Miracles," and in this way he tranquilized the old man's conscience so well that if all the people in the world had told him differently, he would not have believed them.

Once Menico was convinced that the thing had thoroughly set in the old boy's head and that it was not likely to leave it, he struck up another anthem and set out to persuade him not to send Lucia away from his house. It was, he said, a good omen for a place when such accidents came unexpectedly. He told him that in such houses only boys were born, and he told him a thousand other ridiculous stories. He then begged him so strictly, if ever he had any doubt to clear up, to apply always to him, and he would help him most willingly; and he knew so well how to give him reasons that the good old man would not have sold them for any amount of money.

After thanking this learned man and offering him all his fortune, Cecc' Antonio took leave of him. It seemed to him a thousand years before he got back to Tivoli to see if he could beget a boy. As soon as he got home he began the attempt and right nobly his wife did her share, so as not to give the lie to the omen. In due course Lavinia gave birth to a boy, which meant that Lucia remained in the house as long as she liked without the old fellow perceiving or wishing to perceive anything.

* *

*

III

THE DOUBLE CHANGE

THERE LIVED IN THE TIME OF OUR FATHERS A VERY RICH MERCHANT IN FLORENCE NAMED GIROLAMO CAMBINI WHO HAD A WIFE THAT WAS HELD IN HER YOUTH TO BE INCONTESTABLY THE prettiest in the whole town. What was praiseworthy in her above all the rest was her virtue, so that she made a show of placing nothing at a higher price, and far from looking at men, she seemed to be unaware of their existence.

Now it happened that many fellows, after being struck by her extraordinary beauty, finally perceived her cold - ness and, not being able to obtain a single glance from her soon gave up the enterprise. It was, I think, their com - plaints, often heaved to heaven, that convinced Love to take charge of their vengeance.

At this time there lived in Florence a young man of a noble family named Master Pietro dei Bardi, but, since he was a priest who possessed a fine abbey among other benefices, people called him the Abbot. He was univer - sally considered the handsomest fellow in Florence, and I think I remember having seen him when I was a slip of a girl, and as old as he was then, he still seemed very good-looking. Our charming young wife could not, thanks to that lovely form, prevent herself from making a truce with her hard-heartedness and falling madly in love with him; nevertheless, in order not to wander away from her habits, she enjoyed him and his good looks in the depths of her soul without letting anything come to the surface, or she used to talk of him mysteriously with one of her little chambermaids, bred and fed in her father's house, whom she kept for her personal service. In this way she smoth - ered her amorous flames as best she could.

Many and many days had sped by for her in like sufferings, when at last the idea struck her to make shift with her amorous caprice in such a way that neither the Abbot nor anybody else would suspect anything, and here is how. She persuaded her maid Laldomine, that every time she happened to meet the aforesaid Abbot, she should attract his attention by oglings and slight tokens of friendship. She guessed that he would be easily smitten, the more so because the girl was very pretty, having something alluring in her. Besides, her peculiar gar - ments, which were not quite those of a person of condi - tion nor yet those of a servant, imparted an extraordinary grace to her.

One morning, as the two women were at Sante Croce on the occasion of some feast or other, the Abbot hap - pened to be there also, and the cunning little wench put her mistress' recommendations into practice — though quite uselessly — for the Abbot saw or pretended to see nothing, probably because he was still young and not used to such goings-on.

There chanced to be in the Abbot's company another young Florentine named Carlo Sassetti who, having long coveted this Laldomine, noticed her oglings and set about devising some clever trick. He was only waiting for an opportunity, and he immediately put his project into execution.

It so happened that at about this time the husband of the lady, who was named Agnoletta, mounted a horse and set out from Florence for a few days. Carlo, who had an eye open for that, used to do nothing but pass every evening between eight and nine o'clock along the street on which the two women were living. He soon saw Laldomine through a pretty low window on the ground floor near the staircase looking over a little street that was next to the house. Because of the extreme heat the servant was going with a candle in her hand to fetch her mistress some water. Carlo had no sooner caught a glimpse of her than he drew near the window and began in a low voice to call Laldomine; she was quite astonished, but instead of closing the window and going about her business — as anyone would have done who did not wish to listen to idle stories and answer them — she hid the light, came to the window and said, "Who is there?" Carlo quickly an - swered that it was the sweetheart whom she knew very well, and that he wanted to have two words with her.

"What sweetheart do you mean? You had better go about your business, and shame on you. By God's cross! If our men were here you would not act like that. A sign there's no one at home but women! Leave here and bad luck to you, you brazen scamp, before I break my jug over your head!"

Carlo, who had been more than once in such scrapes and knew that the true manner of saying "No" is for us not to lend our ears to the least word of tricksters, was not a bit frightened. Using the sweetest of accents he besought her once more to open the door, saying at the same time that he was the Abbot.

The wench had no sooner heard the Abbot named than she softened down completely and in a chastened tone enquired, "What Abbot? What have I to do with monks and abbots? Begone, begone! If you were an abbot you would not be out at this time of day; I know very well that good priests like he is do not ramble about at night a-whoring after other men's wives, especially to the homes of honest women."

"My Laldomine," Carlo replied, "the great love that I bear you forces me to do what I ought to be on my guard against, but if I come to pester you at such an hour, let it not surprise you. I have so earnest a desire to open my heart to you that there is nothing I would not do for the sake of a few words with you. Have then the goodness, my hope, to let me in, if only for a moment; do not refuse me a thing of such slight importance."

Laldomine felt touched by such entreaties and, thinking that it certainly was the Abbot, she was going to open the door for an instant, but she thought it would be as well to make sure it really was him by means of some understood sign, so she resolved to wait until the following night. She therefore said to him, half in jest, "Be off with you, rascal! Do you think I do not know that you are not the Abbot? If I were quite sure you were he I would let you in, not to do harm, you may be sure, but to find out what you want of me and to tell Girolamo of the fine affronts that you offer him when he is not at home. And if you are not the Abbot? Oh unhappy woman that I should be! I should consider myself the most wretched woman from Borg-Allegri. But come this way tomorrow afternoon at about three o'clock when I will wait for you on the doorstep and, as a sign that it will be you, when you are right in front of the door, blow your nose in this handkerchief." Here she gave him a silk handkerchief with a black border. "Yes, do that," she said, "and I pro - mise that I will let you in. You may then say what you like, anything proper I mean. Do not go and think the contrary."

Then she shut the window in his face without even shaking hands and, running off to her mistress, told her what happened. The lady raised her hands to heaven and, considering the moment had certainly come when her strategem was going to succeed, thanked her with a thou - sand kisses and caresses.

Meanwhile Carlo went home to bed but was unable to sleep a wink thinking of what could be done to make the Abbot give the sign. He got up, wholly absorbed by this problem, and went at about Mass-time to Nunziata where, chancing to meet his friend Girolamo Firenzuola, who generally spent the whole day with the Abbot, he related his adventure of the previous evening and begged his help and advice regarding the sign that he was supposed to give. At once Firenzuola told him to be of good hope and, if that was his only trouble, he could be at peace for he himself would do whatever was needed. After these words he took the handkerchief and left his friend.

When the time seemed appropriate he went to the Abbot and took him for a walk, and passing from one topic to another while strolling along, he led him unsuspectingly by Agnoletta's house. When they were right smack in front of the door, Firenzuola said to the Abbot, previously putting the handkerchief into his hand, "Wipe your nose, old chap, it's all dirty." The Abbot, who thought no more about it, took the handkerchief and blew into it, and Laldomine and Agnoletta firmly believed he had only blown his nose to give the agreed-on sign, and they rejoiced accordingly.

The two young men said no more to each other, and they directed their steps towards Piazza San Giovanni. There Firenzuola asked the Abbot's permission to leave and went off to Carlo who was waiting for him near the Ospedali dei Innocenti. He told him exactly what had taken place and then, bidding him goodbye, he left him alone in his joy.

When night came Carlo went to the house of the two women at about nine o'clock and, setting himself beside the same window as before, waited for Laldomine.

He was not there very long when the servant, prompt - ed by her who was still more eager than Carlo, came to the window, saw him, recognized him as the visitor of yesterday evening and nodded to him to come to the door. Carlo went to the door, and finding it open he entered the house quietly. As soon as he was inside, he wanted to take Laldomine into his arms and kiss her, but she, being faithful to her mistress, would listen to nothing and asked him to stay tranquilly until the Signora had gone to bed. Then pretending that someone was calling her, she left the hall and went off to Agnoletta who was eagerly waiting. When she found out that the Abbot was in her house, if she was not delighted at it, well, I ask you to read on.

Agnoletta had a bed made up with the finest cloths in a room next to the hall and then told Laldomine to go for the Abbot and make him sleep there. The maid groped her way back to Carlo and silently led him into the cham - ber, telling him to take off his clothes and get into bed. She then went out pretending that she was going to see if her mistress was asleep and, before much time had passed,

Signora Agnoletta — well bathed and perfumed — went softly to him instead and in place of Laldomine and got into bed beside him.

Although the darkness contrived to conceal her beauty, her dazzling whiteness was such that it was hard for her to disguise herself. He, believing that he was with Laldomine and she with the Abbot, the two lovers were afraid to converse, and it was by smacks and tight em - braces and all the endearments natural to a lucky couple that they understood each other, making each other the tenderest caresses that you might imagine. If any fond ejaculation chanced to pass their lips, it was murmured so low that the other could not hear it, and, wondering at such discretion, they were only the gladder for it.

But what gives me most mind to laugh when I think of it all is the mutual satisfaction they felt for having arrived at their end by so much amusing drollery. While she was laughing to herself for having so nicely taken him in, he was laughing at her for having been taken in, and they were both so pleased with this fine fun that it enhanced their enjoyment two-fold. Without in the least suspecting who one or the other was, they spent the whole night in such amusement, such rejoicings, and such transports that they could have wished it an eternity long.

When morning dawned Agnoletta got up and, pretending she was going I know not where, she sent Laldomine in her place. She made Carlo dress himself quickly and then let him out secretly by a back door. But that this night that had been the first should not also be the last, they agreed that whenever Girolamo was away they would take advantage of the occasion, and so they often met without anyone being the wiser.

Judge, lovely youths, whether this lady's craft was great. She knew how, under another's name and without risking her honor, to arrange a pleasant journey through life's uncharted seas.

* *
*

IV

THE PENANCE

A LONG TIME AGO THERE LIVED A
PRIEST, CURATE OF SANTA MARIA OF
QUARANTOLA IN THE PISTOIAN MOUNTAINS, AND IN
ORDER TO PRESERVE THE USUAL CUSTOM OF THE
country priests, he fell madly in love with one of his
parishioners. Her name was Tonia and she was the wife
of one of the local big guns, a man named Giovanni, but
better known as Ciarpaglia. This Tonia was perhaps
twenty-two, she was well set up and pretty, and rather
dark owing to the excessive love the sun bore her.
Among other capacities, such as being skilled in nailing
down a base colm and digging a straight furrow, she was
also the best dancer in the place, and if anybody
unfortunately chanced to go through the sets with her,
after the rigadoon, she was so longwinded that she would
put a hundred men out of breath. Happy indeed was he
who could dance a single heat with her, and I can assure
you that she had been the cause of more than one
complaint.

Now when this jolly damsel discovered the clerical
passion, not being in the least intimidated by it, she

occasionally laid herself out to cajole him, and he jumped with joy like a two-year old. He was gnawing into her more and more every day and, without ever speaking of anything below the waist, he would come and chat with her for a couple of hours, telling her the funniest tales you have ever heard. She, who was more cunning than the devil, in order to see if he was very accommodating with folks and if he held out stoutly against the temptation of the purse, always asked him for some little trifle whenever she knew he was going to town, such as two farthings' worth of Levant red, a little ceruse, a buckle for her belt, or some similar bauble. The priest used to spend his money on her as willingly as he would on a church repair. With all this he was waiting, and whether he was satisfied with dressing as a beau for show, by wearing the traditional garb of an angel, and that in Platonic love he found his needs supplied; or whether he was afraid of the husband, or no matter why, he was waiting until she should say to him, "Ser Giovanni, do come to bed with me."

This lasted fully two months, which he spent feeding on the wind, like the clown's donkey, while she made some little profit by him, but things got no farther forward. At length, whether Tonia took it too easy like a woman who is not ashamed to ask him repeatedly for a pair of yellow buskins, those in fashion, split at the sides and laced with a string, then a pair of perforated galoshes with lovely white bridles set off with all sorts of arabesques, or whether it was the urge of Nature, which daily grew more urgent, or for no matter what other motive, he thought it would be well on the first occasion that should present itself and whatever might come of it, to ask her fair and square if there was anything doing.

One day when he saw that she was alone, he brought her a salad from his garden, for he had the finest cabbage lettuce you ever did see, and after giving it to her, he went and sat in front of her and eyed her as well. He then burst into the following speech, "Well, look how pretty she is today, this dear Tonia. By the gospel, I know not what I have not done for you. Oh! You are fairer than the woman on that picture of the temptation of Saint Anthony that Frusino di Meo Puliti recently painted in our church for the salvation of his soul. What lady of Pistoia is as handsome as you? See if those two lips do not resemble the border of my festival chasuble! What joy even to bite them, and the mark of it to remain to vintage-time. Faith, I swear to you by the Seven Virtues of the Mass, if I were not a priest and you not married, I should do what occasion suggests. Oh! the delicious feasts I should make of you! The deuce take it if I should not get rid of the rage that torments my belly!"

While our gentleman was thus holding forth, Tonia remained as though half vexed, with one eye threatening and the other inviting. When he had ended his fine harangue she, while shaking her head, replied, "Ah! Monsignor come, come, you have no need to poke fun at me. If I do not please you, I do not mind so long as I please my husband."

The priest, who already felt sure of the affair, and shook with joy like a wagtail, took heart and continued, "Happy if you pleased me much less, my jewel, for you compel me to follow you about. Oh! What would I not give to be able to touch but once the rosebuds that you have in your bodice. They consume me quicker than a farthing candle before the altar!"

Tonia replied, "Now I wonder what you really would pay? Why you are more niggardly than a cock! Faith, he who names a priest names a beggar and perhaps you didn't mean to spend even a copper! As if I did not know you made a stepmother's face the other day when I asked you for the galoshes! Anybody might think I was asking you for the world and all. I know very well that when your neighbor Mencaglio wanted something from Tentennino's wife, he jolly well had to pay half the price of that petticoat she had made for All Saints' Day. And you know enough about petticoats to know that that wasn't bought for nothing."

"By the body of Saint Nothingatall, my dear Tonia," cried the priest, "you are a thousand times wrong, for I am more open-handed with women that anyone else I know, and I never go to town without spending at least two bolognini with the pretty ladies who live behind the Prior's Palace. That being so, think of what I would do for you with your lovely figure! You have so stirred up my liver and tripes that I have no longer any leisure to dispatch a mouthful of the Office, to tell you the truth, I fear you have enchanted me."

Hearing such fine promises, the cunning dame wished to try him, and so she told him that she would be happy to give herself to him for his pleasure, provided that he would bind himself to buy her a pair of wide yellow serge sleeves edged with green velvet, also green ribbons that they tie in their hair and let float about in the air, a green hair net with its ear-knot and, besides, to lend her three bolognini for a piece of linen from the weaver's. If not, he had only to return to his pretty ladies who served him so well for his two bolognini.

The poor priest, whose clapper was quite ready for the bell, unwilling to lose so fine an opportunity, promised her not only the sleeves, but the petticoat with an under one as well; and he wanted straightway to join battle, when she, seeming rather to enjoy the flirting exclaimed, "Oh, Oh! Dom Giovanni, my darling, just look and see if you have not by chance a few odd coppers in your pocket, I am very hard up and, believe me, my old man hasn't a rag of a shirt to put on his back."

The good priest would have preferred to have been granted credit, and he tried to make out that he was a bit short, but that when Complines were ended, he would go straight to the church and look in the candle boxes to see if there was enough in them to make up the amount and, if so, he would let her have the cash at once. But Tonia, noticing how he was imposing on her, pretended she was vexed and said to him in a sour tone of voice, "Did I not say you are as mean as they make them? Clear out! By the Cross, you shall not lay a hand on me till you have shelled out. I'm taking a lesson out of the book of you priests. You will not sing unless you get paid on the nail! It suffices, I think, if I am willing to wait for the rest until you have been to town, but a trifle on account I must have, for I do not know which way to turn for a penny."

"Look here now, do not get angry, my Toniotta; I will just see whether by any possible chance I have some money on me." After saying this, he pulled out of his breeches pocket a small purse full of holes from which he laboriously squeezed out a few coppers which, with many a wry grimace, he paid over one by one. No sooner was it done than she, all merry, led him away to a nearby barn to help him chime his bells a bit. And there they met more than once until he went to Pistoia.

When he was about to return, whether he had lost his memory or was grieved to spend his money, at any rate he only bought the net, which he took her and apologized because he had forgotten the sleeves at home. He prom - ised to bring them the next day, and he knew so well how to wheedle her that, taking the net, she was still pleased to chime the triple bob-major. But one day and another passed and the mean old scamp brought neither sleeves nor cuffs.

Tonia began to be vexed and one fine evening let fly at him with a few complimentary remarks. He who had pretty fairly shaken the donkey's bridle, thinking that if she wanted sleeves she had only to buy them, replied to her so briskly that she was highly displeased with him and resolved to avenge herself. "Away, away, you petticoated swindler," said she to herself, while still reproaching herself for her folly. "If I don't make you sit up for it, may a fever burn me up! I have been silly to entangle myself with so despicable a brood, as if you had not heard it said a thousand times that they are all of the same savor, but let it rest there for now."

To show her anger better, she would not even look at him for three or four days. Then, in order to more easily avenge herself on him according to the scheme she had conceived, she began again to coax him with provoking words and, without speaking about the sleeves, pretended she had made peace with him.

One day, when the moment seemed propitious for the execution of her plan, she called him to her and told him how her Ciarpaglia had gone to Cutigliano and begged him, if he wished to treat himself to an agreeable pleasure with her, to come to the house for her about None, when she would be alone and expecting him. If by chance he did not find her in to kindly wait a bit as she would soon be back.

Ask not whether Dom Caprone felt happy at such a request; he stood in his slippers, saying to himself, "I must say I was surprised at her being so long about falling in love with me. You can see the sleeves haven't bothered her much. I was a fool to give her anything at all; it would have been all the same by now. I'll tell you what, Dom Giovanni, if you don't get more than your money's worth now, I shall think you're the biggest fool ever."

While thus talking to himself, he waited for the appointed hour, and it had no sooner come than he did as the woman had bidden him. The minx had that morning related to her husband how the priest had more than once solicited her for her virtue, and the present arrangement was agreed on by them in order to inflict a severe chastisement on the priest.

As soon as the woman perceived Dom Giovanni entering, she beckoned to Ciarpaglia and one of his brothers who were watching out for this moment and preceding them softly went off for the gallant who was already on the bed with his feet in the air. Dom Giovanni had no sooner espied her than, without doubting anything, he went to meet her. Saluting her politely, he tried to throw his arms around her neck and kiss her in the French fashion; but he had hardly time to accost her when Ciarpaglia appeared, crying like a madman, "Ah! You whoremonger of a priest — you shaven pate! Wait, wait till I drop on you! Is that the way a pious priest behaves, eh? May God heap calamities on you, you beggar's brat! Go and herd swine! Be off to the sty and not to the church, you hypocrite!" Then turning aside to the brother in a rage that had no equal he continued, "Don't hold me back — let me get at him — or I will do you an injury. Leave it to me! I'll bloody my wife and eat this traitor's heart red hot, red hot!"

While the man was raving like this the priest, breech-fouled, had slunk in a funk beneath the bed and yelled for mercy with all his might. But it was so much chaff thrown against the wind because Ciarpaglia was fully determined that for once it should be the layman who would impose penance on the priest. He had in this very room a large chest which had lain there since the time of his great grandfather and in which his wife kept the best of her clothes. He opened it, flung out all the gewgaws and, dragging the priest from under the bed, made him pull his breeches down, which the latter had, while waiting for Tonia, already unlaced, not to let her languish too long, I guess. He seized his testicles, which were stout and of fair length, as befitted a gallant, put them into the chest, nailed down the lid, then with a big key stuffed up the keyhole and, having got his brother to give him an old notched razor, he laid this on the chest without a word of explanation and then went off to his work.

The unfortunate priest, thus left in the state you may imagine, felt such pain at first that he was likely to faint. Fortunately the lock was so dislocated that the bolt scarcely entered the hasp, and there was a gap between the lid and the box, so at first our hero came to no great harm. Nevertheless, every time he caught sight of the razor and thought of the place where he had been seized, such agony pressed on his heart that he wondered he was not yet dead; had he not forced himself to keep at his ease a while in saying to himself that they only wanted to frighten him and that before long they would be coming to free him from this torture, I believe he would have been really dead.

After he had remained pretty long undecided between doubt and hope, seeing nobody was coming to his aid, and his flesh was beginning to swell — causing him consider - able pain — he started to cry for help. No one came. Then he attempted to break the lock. The only result was to tire himself and increase the pain in the tumefying flesh. He then stopped exciting himself and began to implore assistance.

Assistance did not come, mercy was absent, and the pain got worse and worse. Despairing of getting safely out of the affair, he took hold of the razor on the firm resolution to end such agony, even at the cost of his life, but straightway seized with a cowardly weakness and compassion for himself, he cried out while weeping, "Oh my God! What have I done to deserve this? Cursed be Tonia and the first day I ever set eyes on her!" Then oppressed by an inexpressible torment, he became silent.

Some time after, he fixed his eyes on the razor, took hold of it again and, slightly grazing the skin, tried how it hurt him; but he had hardly drawn it near when there came over him such a cold sweat, a dread, a swoon, that he felt himself fainting off. No longer knowing what to do, worn out by fatigue, he lay on his belly across the chest, and while now whining, now sighing, now yelling, now offering himself to God, now blaspheming, the pain exasperated him and became so acute that, being no longer able to bear it, he saw himself forced to use the only means that remained for his deliverance. Making a virtue of necessity, he grasped the razor, exercised on himself the vengeance of Ciarpaglia and separated himself from his privy parts. The operation caused him so ter -

rible a pain that he dropped down half dead and bellowed like a wounded bull. The folks that Ciarpaglia had care - fully gathered came running at this noise and they tended the priest so that he escaped with his life — if it can be called living to be deprived of the mainstay of life.

* *
*

V

THE TEMPTATION OF THE FLESH

THERE WAS, AND STILL IS TODAY, AT PERUGIA, A VERY RICH CONVENT CROWDED WITH PERUGIAN LADIES WHO, FOR WANT OF KNOWING MY EXCELLENT RECIPE FOR LIFE, STRAYED FROM THE rule of Saint Benedict, their father.

Most of the nuns, perhaps all, being thoroughly in accord with the abbess, occupied themselves only in procuring those pleasures that the want of a dowry, their fathers' greed, their mothers' preferences, the step - mothers' jealousy or other similar accidents had deprived them of, and they had carried these pleasures to such a pitch that one might easily find virtue everywhere, save in this holy retreat. The bishop was therefore obliged far more by the complaints that the folks of the place had frequently made to him, than by any vigilance or solicitude on his part, to find some remedy against their disorderly life. He therefore ordered part of them, chiefly those who, grown old in wickedness, were but little fit to enter on a new life, to be sent away. He kept the rest and added to them a certain number of girls, as well as those chosen from other convents of purer morals.

Among the latter was a venerable matron who had lived for more than forty years in the convent of Monte Lucci with an odor of sanctity, and he appointed her as abbess. By means of new rules and a good example she at length brought the house to a suitable observance.

This abbess had ordered among other prescriptions that, between None and Vespers, at the chiming of a hundred bells that she took the greatest care to have rung, the nuns should be bound to take themselves to the chapel, or their cells, or wherever they liked best and to remain there one-half hour in prayer, to beseech the good Lord to remove them from all evil temptations. The one she saw putting most fervor in this practice, the abbess considered to be of better will in living well than any other, believing she was not mistaken, that the sting of the flesh once mastered, all the rest would be easy.

But because the outcome of violence does not last long, and pestilent water easily spreads again over its former bed. It turned out that among the ones who had remained, this certain Sister Appellagia, both young and pretty, could no longer endure to have simply prayers and the sound of bells in order to satisfy her already corrupted appetite. Previous to the reforms she had fallen in love with a young man of Perugia who was noble and very rich, and who enjoyed great favor with Giovan-Paolo Baglione. He too loved her exceedingly, and they had so well known how to act that they were often together in the nun's cell for three or four hours at a time, and jolly hours all! This was done so secretly that it was impossible for anyone to notice it. She could not, however, for fear of giving the alarm, remain locked up with him all day long in her room, as she would have wished — and besides she was obliged to keep with the other sisters in the convent for the usual exercises of the house — but, as soon as she heard the blessed bell, she ran quickly to her cell under pretext of this prayer, so quickly that she seemed to be going up to paradise. The abbess, who had never sus - pected anything, seeing her so exact in this intention, had conceived the highest opinion of her.

Now it so happened one day that one of the ancient nuns, having gone into the garden to gather a little salad to be sent to some relation, heard the temptation bell ring. She feared, however, that the messenger might go away without the salad and decided to go on filling her basket and to let the prayer slide. Tidings of this misdeed were immediately carried to the abbess who, having called the delinquent to her, made an incredible row about it. Great God! Among the other things she said to her, and what stung her most, was that she should take as a model Sister Appellagia, who never found herself so busy in anything no matter how important, but she very quickly left it the moment she heard that bell ringing.

When the nun, who was perhaps better acquainted with the young brood of the convent than the abbess, saw herself reproached by the example of Sister Appellagia, she would listen no further and all in a rage she said to herself, "To be sure, I must indeed see where so much fervor and devotion comes from. There is something fishy at the bottom of it, oh! yes, and I shall just go and find out what she does in her cell. Only let tomorrow come, and I'll make the whole convent laugh." While speaking to herself in this way, and pregnant with an evil will, she waited until the next day for the temptation bell to ring. The moment having come, the cursed nun, as soon as she saw Sister Appellagia running to her cell in order to flee the temptation, softly drew near the door, made a hole in a certain opening, which was covered inside with a sheet of paper, and discovered how the learned young damsel had found true means of freeing herself from temptation. Without making the slightest noise, she went off full of glee to the abbess, told her how things stood, and took her to see the game of back - gammon. I could never describe to you the intense pain and trouble that the poor abbess felt on hearing so hideous a story, for it seemed to her indeed that she had wasted her time and pains in effecting so many reforms. Fired with rage, she went to Appellagia's cell, burst open the door and beholding with her very eyes what she had probably never dreamt of before, she nearly collapsed with grief. Turning to the little nun, she called her the grossest names that were ever addressed to a woman of this kind taken in a similar case. "This was then, you devil's brat, the motive of your devotion! It was for this you showed yourself so prompt in running to your cell, you nasty barefaced baggage! So the teachings inculcated in you, the warnings given you and the new reforms have all produced this fine fruit! Is it for this that I left Monte Lucci, to be witness of such ignominy, to behold with my own two eyes within the space of two months what I have not even imagined in thought in forty years! God grant that I stay here no longer where the devil has so much power and audacity!"

Having addressed these words and many more to the young girl, she turned to upbraid the man and warn him what his end would be if he did not quickly turn from his evil ways. Returning then to the sister she added, "On this one, the profligate, I shall inflict such a chastisement as will fit so enormous a crime." But Appellagia, who was beginning to grow tired of these reproaches, could bear them no longer and, displaying a countenance that would have made one say, "She is indeed beautiful and good," spoke in this manner, "Madam, you make much ado about nothing and in my opinion you are a thousand times wrong. Tell me, please, why you have prescribed that every day at the sound of the bell we offer up a private orison, if it be not that every one of us be delivered from the temptation of the flesh? What better means could you invent than the one that I have discovered myself? What other road could we take that would give such rest and peace? The prayers and acts of your invention only strengthen our temptations, whereas by my method I can get to sleep with my mind as free from naughty fancies as I sincerely hope yours is. Anyhow, to cut a long story short, either allow me to preserve myself from temp - tation as I understand things, or give me leave to go where I think fit; for my part I do not intend to trouble the ears of the Lord by day, only to find myself tempted and tormented all through the night."

The abbess, on hearing her give so impudent an an - swer, considered that it would be better policy and more profitable to the convent to pack her off than to keep her against her will. The young man also begged the nun's release, and this convinced the abbess. She at once gave the nun permission to quit the convent and the sooner the better. And on that very same night the little strumpet went off to sleep at the young man's house, and she delivered herself from the temptation of the flesh during many months, nor did she need to wait for the warning sound of a bell.

* *
*

VI

THE TWO FRIENDS

MANY YEARS AGO THERE LIVED IN FLORENCE TWO YOUNG MEN OF HIGH DESCENT AND GREAT WEALTH, THE ONE NAMED LAPO TORNAQUINCI, THE OTHER NICCOLO DEGLI ALBIZI, who had, from earliest boyhood, contracted so close a friendship that one would have fancied they could only live together.

They had been living thus for ten years, when Niccolo's father departed from this life, leaving his son more than thirty thousand ducats' worth of goods, and, as Lapo was in need of a hundred ducats, Niccolo not only obliged him with the amount without even waiting to be asked for it but begged him to consider himself a part-owner of the fortune. These were tokens indeed of a truly noble and virtuous soul, worthy of causing the highest hopes to be conceived, had not the too emancipated youthfulness, naturally prone to evil, the wealth acquired without work, and the somewhat unpraiseworthy habits, engaged him in a wicked life. Indeed, as he followed the example of those who at night go to bed poor and rise in the morning rich, after having drudged in misery, he

soon had round him a gang of fellows of so depraved a
life that they would have removed the aureola from the
greatest saint's head. Those keeping company with him,
now at dinner, now at supper, taking him to such and such
a feast or to the house of some lost woman, made him
squander so much money that it really was shameful. On
seeing this, his friend, Lapo, being a very sober and
reserved young man, was grieved to the bottom of his
heart and all day long was behind him to recall him to
righteousness, to rebuke him for his wrong acts, as their
friendship demanded. But all was in vain. The new
cronies had, with their dishonorable pastimes and perni -
cious counsels, more sway over him than Lapo and his
wise warnings. These fellows, who were watching Lapo,
related so much evil to Niccolo about him and denounced
him to such a degree that, having begun by detaching
himself from him, he ended by fleeing from him, thus
intimating that he intended to live in his own way. Lapo,
when once sure of the fact, ceased through weariness
from being always after him and let him conduct himself
as he pleased. The upshot was that the poor fool, continu -
ing to live as he ought not to do, saw an event befall him
that he did not expect.

Just at that time there was in Florence a handsome and
graceful young widow of pleasing manners who, having
contracted the habit, even during the lifetime of her
husband, of preferring money to honor, without casting a
further thought on the family in which she was born or
that into which she had entered by marriage — both being
of great nobility — she easily gratified young men with
her love, provided they were not only fine fellows in
appearance but were flush with money and generous.
Both before and during her widowhood, she had plucked

more than one pigeon clean, though passing for a second Saint Bridget in the eyes of her relatives.

At the first news she had of Niccolo's fortune and the pace he was going, she at once founded great projects for him and, having secured an introduction, began to pretend she was smitten by him. Then, as though she could no longer conceal her infatuation, she set to entice him night and day with letters and messengers. I have no need to tell you whether Niccolo, who had been persuaded by his cronies that he was a fair devil with the ladies, was pleased or not. Happy was he who could stick in his little word to flatter him, to congratulate him on his latest conquest and extol the lady to the skies! More than one dinner was wheedled out of him over this affair, and they wound up so well that nothing else would suit him any longer than discussing the lady's charms with these precious rascals. Since she knew how to get round him so nicely, while pretending she was dying of love, she succeeded in finding herself alone with him to do what she had already done with many others.

Being pretty and having a way about her, she knew how to make a man dote on her better than any strut who had spent twenty years on her greens, sometimes using the mildest expressions in the world, sometimes the harshest, today feigning she is unable to live any longer without him, she loved him so much, and tomorrow making him jealous with a new sweetheart, warning him that the moment was come to wed her, then wishing it no longer, banging her door in his face, again running after him, at another time pretending to be big with child, she so exasperated the poor wretch that he completely lost his bearings. All other things had gone out of his head. His affairs remained at random, the new friends, as well as the old were thrown aside; diversions, games, suppers, were all, all of her, when she wished and as she wished them. From the moment she perceived that the bird had no further need of being tamed, she set her mind on clipping his wings so that he could not fly away, and she succeeded in it pretty well, not only estranging Lapo, who was his true friend, but creating mischief in the hearts of his other good-time friends who had themselves thrown him into her clutches. And it seemed to them that all that the pretty lady had racked out of Niccolo came from their purses, and they were quite right, for the strut finally reduced him by her craft and intrigues to such an extremity that, far from being able to give them a dinner or a supper, he had not enough money left to feed himself.

When he saw to what state he had come, he recognized how much better he would have done by lending an ear to the advice of Lapo than listening to the flatteries of his new favorites, and he realized besides what a wretched end the love of these women always has, who offer the pleasures of their bodies to the first comer, not indeed through tender affection, but for greed of gain. Lucrezia — I now remember the lady's name — seeing that his crown pieces were beginning to be missing and that he would soon run out, nevertheless knew how to carry her mock love to the end; she then began to assume such manners with him that he could very well perceive how dimly her fire was blazing.

But what pained him most was the discovery of a new amorous caprice in his mistress. She had recently learned that a certain Simone Davizi had, by his father's death, become very wealthy, and she fell in love with him at once and to such a degree that she completely forgot Niccolo. A wise, prudent and fortunate young woman, truly! She knew so well how to read one's eyes and instruct one's heart that she discovered beauty among men in proportion to the amount of gold or silver she saw, and she felt most love when she heard coins jingle.

Niccolo clearly saw that his affairs were going from bad to worse, and that he was being treated ignominiously by her whom he had cherished more than his life; but, far from decreasing in ratio to these outrages, his love, or more properly his rage, increased day by day. He longed to be with her as in the past, and finding no chance for it, he thundered against himself and her. He did not know what to set his mind on, and his state inspired pity. The pals of his gay time had come with his fortune, and with it they had vanished. His relations would see him no more, his neighbors laughed at him, and strangers used to mock him.

Having well and duly considered all this on several occasions, he fell into such despair that he deliberated, as a last resource, on putting an end to such suffering by some horrible death, and perhaps he would have put his idea into execution, had he not, while recalling to mind the close friendship that united him to Lapo, and considering it a sure thing that the latter would not have lost the memory of so tender an affection, thought it well to go and see him, leaving aside all false shame, to relate to him his mishap and to beg his pardon for God's sake. He therefore went to him without more ado and did what he had resolved on.

Lapo, who had, as they say, let three loaves pass for a couple, being unable to prevent it, did not fail to take pity on Niccolo, seeing him — according to his own acknowl - edgements — plunged into a more complete ruin that he would have supposed. He was greatly afflicted by it and knowing that his friend was in more need of help than counsel, said kindly to him, "Niccolo, I do not wish to act like those who, after having warned their friend to no purpose, reproach him with not having listened to their advice. Those, I think, seek only to glorify themselves in blaming whoever has not lent an ear to their warnings. You are aware that when I saw you entering into the way that led you to where I would rather you were not, I ful - filled the duty of a friend with my words. Now that you are arrived at the end, it is not words that any longer suffice, and I mean not to fail by my acts in the same duty. I shall act as if I shall undergo penance, sweet penance in - deed, since it will give me the opportunity of showing what my heart is to my friend. The duty I wish to fulfill is as laudable and worthy of recommendation as it has al - ways been, but very few men have discharged it, and this is the clearest proof of its merit; I too desire to be reck - oned among this small number and, leaving words aside, wish to show you the effects. Come therefore with me."

Without another word he took him into his room, and opening his money box gave him a sum by which Niccolo might judge how much he loved him. He then exhorted him by kind words to be of good cheer and made him understand that, when this money was spent, he would not fail to supply him with more, as much and as often as he wanted.

After making so generous a present and giving him such bright hopes for the future, Lapo began in a most friendly tone to criticize his past life, to censure his connection with that woman; and these words had such influence over Niccolo that, if they did not dislodge her at once from his thoughts, they nevertheless infused into his heart a certain regret for what he had done and excited a certain shame in him. He still loved the woman and still longed for an occasion to slake his passion.

But the treacherous female was not long before finding that he was in funds again; conjecturing that everything had turned out to her greater advantage and not wishing to let him slip from her, she began a second time to importune him with letters, and so frequently too that Niccolo was obliged to let himself be locked in her arms again. She persuaded him that he was finer than ever; and that she more than ever wished him well; that all that had sprung up between them was no fault of hers, but of some relation or maid; that the very great love he bore her, that love that often causes the surest thing to go awry, had made him jealous about a thing that was far from being true; and she knew so nicely how to fool the poor devil that she squeezed many crown pieces out of him.

And she would have had all his money had it not haply come to pass — as his cruel destiny would have it — that one night among others, while he was with her and had fallen asleep, she heard by certain understood signs her new lover passing outside. Allured by her evil genius, she persuaded herself that Niccolo had, as they say, tied the ass to the right peg, and she longed to go as far as the door to amuse herself a while with the other. She got up, threw a light covering over her shoulders, went down very quietly to the back door and invited her lover in. One word leads to another; from words to deeds is easy going; they thought they were safe, since Niccolo was so deeply asleep, and they stayed far longer than they should have.

Niccolo woke up just in the middle of the affair and, not finding Lucrezia beside him was greatly surprised. He called her several times and, getting no answer, guessed the truth. He immediately jumped to his feet, dressed himself as best he could while groping in the dark, and, having stuck a sword in his belt, crept silently up to them.

Before either of the guilty pair noticed anything, he was at their pillow and, beholding them stretched on sacks of flour, he was all of a sudden carried off with such wrath, such madness, that, without thinking of what he was doing, he drew his sword and dealt both of them at once with such a well-directed cut that he almost loped off Simone's head, while grievously wounding the woman's arm. Then his ire only increased, he redoubled his cuts and only stopped when he saw that they both lay dead.

All the inhabitants came running at this commotion, they began to bewail the amiable young woman, and each one had his word to stick in. As for Niccolo, as if he made no question about the crime he had committed, he walked out of the house satisfied that he had performed a great feat. Still mad with fury and still grasping his reeking sword, he was running to Lapo's house, quite delighted to go and have a laugh over this fine exploit, when he just ran into a squadron of the Bargello who, seeing him running in such a manner, surmised he was guilty of some crime and dragged him off to jail. There, without any need of pressuring or torturing him, he confessed how the thing had happened and, found guilty of manslaughter, was sentenced to death.

But his generous friend decided that this was the moment to show what the greatness, the strength, of friendship may be. He did so much with the aid of his friends and money that he saved Niccolo's life for him. The punishment was commuted to banishment for life to Barletta in Apulia. That did not satisfy Lapo. He con - demned himself to exile too and forsaking his sweet and pleasant country, went to live with Niccolo in a wretched land where he supplied his wants out of his private fortune. He brought back the wandering mind of his friend to the study of literature and other worthy occupations, and they both gained the esteem of the king of the country. In the course of time, he obtained leave for Niccolo to live at Naples, and there the two friends lived until Niccolo's death, when Lapo had him taken to Florence and buried among his relatives. He also ordered that after his own death he was to be buried in the same grave so that in death, as in life, they should not be divided.

* *
*

VII

THE SEWED-UP BRIDE

THERE STILL LIVED IN FLORENCE, NOT MANY MONTHS AGO, A CERTAIN ZANOBI DI PIERO DEL CIMA, ONE OF THOSE GOOD CHRISTIANS WHO RECOMMEND THEMSELVES TO THE CRUCIFIX OF San Giovanni, Chiarito or San Pier del Murrone. He had somewhat more confidence in the Annunciation of San Marco than in that of the Servites, and he used to say it was older and quainter. He gave other reasons for his preference, such as, the angel's profile was sharper, the dove whiter and other similar motives. I know he let himself be carried off more than once to severely upbraid the prior because he did not keep it veiled, stating that nothing had given so great a reputation to that of the Servites and the Cintola of Prato, as showing them with much ado and many ceremonies.

With all that he was a fine fellow. He often went to confession, fasted every Friday, assisted at Complines on all festival days and, when he made vows to these Crucifixes, he observed them as scrupulously as grocers weigh pepper, even though it clearly cost him money, for in all he spent on them at least a third of his income. In this way, without wife or children, he lived an easy and comfortable life with an old woman who was in his house for forty years.

Now this good old man desired to cut a figure among the consuls of his Guild, and he made a vow to the Crucifixes that were in the Oratory of the Servites that if he obtained this dignity he would give a hundred pounds in silver to some lass as a dowry. His vow was heard, and this was surely a great miracle for the Crucifixes had not even yet been painted!

The simpleton had no sooner heard the news of his election that, quite overwhelmed with joy and eager for compliments, he gave an account of his vow to his confessor, a certain Ser Giulano Bindi, rector of San Remo and a reputed saint. The priest mentioned to him a certain Monna Mechera da Calenzano of whom folks had whispered I know not what implicating the priest himself. But I should affirm nothing about it on that account, for it is a sin to think evil of monks and especially of those who hear confessions, who say Mass with downcast eyes, and who have the care of souls, as well as the affairs of widows. Suffice it to say that he bore her affection and every time she came to Florence she stayed at his house.

He informed her of what was in the air, and she set off at once in search of Zanobi and entreated him for God's sake to give the money to a daughter of hers who was ripe for marriage but penniless. Thanks to the cleric's assist - ance and her own clever coaxings, the silly fellow gave her a written promise, stating therein that as soon as a marriage was settled he would hand over a hundred pounds in hard cash. It has been asserted that he gave the woman no document, but simply promised by word of mouth, and that he gave the husband the writing later on.

This is more likely and agrees better with what you are going to see. Be the truth then as it may, and let each understand it as he will. I want no reproaches.

The gay old woman, once in possession of the promise, returned home quite merry and set herself to marry off her daughter. By the aid of her devoted priest she found a suitable husband; but he, as soon as they had shaken hands — whether he had as a pledge the written engagement of Zanobi or whether he received it from the mother-in-law, after giving his word and the ring — was obliged to set out and spend a few weeks at Chianti on business, and he left intending to celebrate the wedding on his return.

It turned out that he was detained much longer than he had thought, so much so that Monna Mechera believed he would not come back. She was tempted to do a very funny thing and to even get hold of the hundred pounds. How she worked her daughter up to it and what her own end could really be I cannot easily imagine. Suffice it to say that she cast her eyes upon her neighbor, a certain big booby about twenty-five years of age, although this fellow was a bit of a rake on the quiet. His name was Menicuccio dalle Prata.

One day the woman took him aside and said, "Menicuccio, whenever you wish to do me a great favor, without its costing you anything, without your running any risk, you will be the means of my getting a hundred pounds as easily as picking them up in the street and at the same time you will save my Sabatina from going bad. And here's how! A Florentine has promised me that when my daughter has married he will give her a hundred pounds as a dowry and, as you are aware, I have betrothed her to Giannella del Mangano who has since gone to the end of the earth and who has sent word that he will not return to get married unless I first send him the money. But the donor will not part with the cash until the girl is married, so I do not know what course to take, and meanwhile Sabatina suffers. To tell you the truth, I am heartily sick of it, and for some time now I have felt uneasy, seeing all day messing around here certain men I would not like to trust. You know what it is if a girl is pretty and there is no man in the house. Folks respect nothing. So much the worse for the poor. I should like you to assist me in getting hold of this money, and it would be easy if you will give your mind to it. First I will make you a present of a beautiful brand new shirt with quilted wrist bands and embroidered collar, the finest to be seen in the district. Then I shall also give you the money to buy yourself a new pair of shoes and a cap."

Imagine whether Menicuccio cocked his ears at such fine offers. He replied to Monna Mechera, "Faith if this thing is possible, coming in on the ground floor! Any - thing so long as I don't get pinched."

"Eh! Fool!" replied Monna Mechera, "what do you say? Do you think I would let you run the slightest risk? God forbid! Do you know what I want? I want you to pretend you are my daughter's husband."

"Oh! You want me to pose as your son-in-law? But everybody knows who he is."

"Yes, here, but not in Florence. The three of us will go there, you calling yourself Giannella, and you will tell this Florentine that you wish to get married at once. As he has never seen you before, he will believe you are the bridegroom and will count you out the money. You will then hand it over to me, and I shall thus be able to compel Giannella to keep his promise. Otherwise I can see the job hanging on a twelve-month."

The thing seemed easy enough to Menicuccio, were it not that he feared the Florentine must know him; but the woman understood so well how to get around him that he finally agreed and said, "All right. I've had harder jobs anyhow. But look here, you will have to pay me a carlino a day while the farce lasts, to make up for the time I lose from work."

Agreeing, the woman took him home, and they talked the matter over with the girl and arranged their plans. Early the next morning they set out for Florence.

Some people pretend that the young lass, who was all there, seeing in Menicuccio a big blond blockhead, a fellow fit to make one feeble and safe as a eunuch, conceived the idea of enjoying herself. Others say that he cared far more about the girl than he did about Monna Mechera's promises. While showing himself a jovial clown, he was, as we say, a thorough blackguard who had played many dirty tricks. However, I affirm nothing, though I rather fancy he was a bit of both.

They went off therefore, as I was saying, in search of Zanobi, who was just walking out from Laud in Or San Michele, and they told him how they were coming for the hundred pounds, because the husband, Menicuccio, so they said, wished to lead the bride to the altar next Tuesday — it now being Saturday — and they intended to buy a bed at the Monday market, and so on and so forth.

The old man had arrived back the previous evening from Riboja, where he had been visiting a small demense that he intended to purchase. He received them most kindly and told them he was wholly at their disposal, but he wanted so see the girl married with his own eyes and in no way would he allow himself to be played with. Con - sequently it would be his pleasure to invite them to supper and to lend them a bed and dispose of everything that would be necessary in order that the marriage might be consummated in his house on the following night. Of course they agreed.

They went the next morning, which was Sunday, to the wedding Mass as man and wife, and in the evening they dined at Zanobi's table and abandoned themselves to all the gaiety and diversion usual in similar cases between newly married couples to the great joy of Zanobi, who congratulated himself on having been the means of such a charming union. He even hoped that his deed would bring him further good luck.

When they had all eaten their fill, and bedtime had arrived, he made the young couple understand that they were to go and sleep in a room halfway up the house where he usually let his farmer sleep whenever he came to bring him a basket of apples. He told Monna Mechera that she would sleep with his old servant, but she wanted to be in the same room as her daughter. He explained how unlawful this was, and he would tolerate it on no account.

She held her peace, not wishing to create any suspicion in his mind, but she called Sabatina to her and taking her aside, preached her a long sermon face to face telling her that she should take precious good care not to let Menicuccio sew his beans in the drills of Monte Ficale. Not contented with what the cunning wench promised and swore her twenty times over, she sewed her up in her chemise from head to toe with a double thread, so that it was impossible to get her out. She next called Menicuccio and, after making him swear that he would conduct himself as with his own sister, she put the couple to bed and then went off to her own room.

The bridegroom and bride had not been more than half an hour in bed when, whether the warmth of the blankets or the itching of a little scab which Sabatina felt tickling her between her thighs, or whether she wished to pee, or no matter why, she set about looking for the means of ripping her chemise, and she struggled so hard with her hands and her feet that she worked herself entirely out of it. The poor boy, whose conscience was perhaps pricking him for being in such a place, began by stretching out his legs and throwing out his arms as one does on waking. Then, perceiving the change, as by mere chance, he laid his hands on the girl. She was undoubtedly a bad bedfellow, for she set to tumbling over his side. He did as much and they were soon in each other's arms. Menicuccio, being the stronger, rolled over on top and stormed the imminent breach. Then thinking he had per - haps done wrong and wishing to make peace he began to kiss her and embrace her, but since she seemed cross with him, he charged to the assault once more. Eight times did he renew the charge, till Sabatina, taking the offensive, dragged him underneath her and squeezed him so tightly that he had to cry out. She too had cause for whining and began to weep. Nevertheless, she had done battle so boldly that I cannot think that it was her first engagement.

At length the hour for rising came, and when Monna Mechera saw that the chemise was ripped, that the outlaws had violated their ban and passed through Hollow Street butchery, she felt like kicking up a row, then, inspired by a better thought, in order not to disclose the plot, and knowing besides that she found what she was looking for, held her peace as best she could and, turning to Menicuccio, besought him for God's sake not to say a word to a soul.

Without further discussion, as soon as they were dressed, they went to Zanobi who was waiting for them by the kitchen fire, where he was explaining what the Flower of Virtue meant to his old servant. The gay old dog wished them "Good morning" and "Many happy returns," gave them a good breakfast, then handed them the money done up in a handkerchief. He next gave them his blessing, begging them to visit him from time to time, then packing them off home and letting them take the written engagement with them.

They returned all merry and bright to Calenzano, and to compensate Menicuccio the old woman allowed him to interview her daughter. For, since he had his hands in the dough, she fancied that one does not soil the trough more to make ten loaves than one.

This state of things lasted perhaps two months, until Giannella, the true husband, came back. Shortly after his return, he resolved to conclude the marriage, and without consulting the mother-in-law, which was the cause of all the wrangling, went to Florence. He met Zanobi who was just hearing Mass at the altar of the Virgin in Santa Maria del Campo and, after many twists and turns, asked him for the hundred pounds.

At this request, without answering a word, Zanobi burst out laughing, thinking that this was a joke, but Giannella began to bawl out that honest men do not give their word and deny it afterward and that if his money was not counted out to him, he well knew where to go and see justice done him. Zanobi, deviating for once from his habits, was forced into a fury and replied with a stream of insults like any other man. "You rascal, you robber, where do you think you are? In the street perhaps? Three months ago Monna Mechera, Sabatina and her husband came to see me and in my house, under my nose, consum - mated the marriage with all the usual ceremonies.

"I handed them the money myself, and now this thief comes and asks for it again. It is true I forgot to get back my agreement. I gave it no thought. I did not suspect that anyone would attempt such a trick. This man must have stolen it from them. Fortunately for me I entered it in my book. I took note of everything; and you cannot catch me, wretch. If you do not get out of my sight I shall lodge a complaint and have you treated as you deserve."

On seeing his bad humor, Giannella went straight to the Episcopal Palace and had Zanobi summoned. He presented himself, related to the vicar how the thing had taken place, and the vicar ordered Monna Mechera, her daughter and Menicuccio to appear. Through them we learned all, even to the story of the chemise, and how Sabatina won the final round.

The vicar's sentence was that the old hag should be flogged, that Menicuccio should give Giannella forty pounds, which had been spent, and that Giannella should take Sabatina to his own home and ask no questions about her doings with Menicuccio. This latter, in order to find the forty pounds was obliged to sell his land. They say the vicar gave this judgement because he had faked the marriage Mass, but I do not think so. He had really married them and it is wrong to suggest otherwise. He proved what *Futuro caret* means, an adage which signifies that the fruit or rather the first-crop cost poor Menicuccio dearly. But he who possesses once for all does not always suffer!

* *
*

VIII

THE PRECIOUS JEWEL

SHOULD ANYBODY SAY THEY HAVE JUST CAUGHT A FOX, YOU WOULD NOT CRY OUT "A MIRACLE!" REMEMBERING THE PROVERB, "FOXES ALSO ALLOW THEMSELVES TO BE TAKEN," YOU WOULD be more inclined to think that the dexterity of some man or the courage of some animal had put the beast in this fix. But if you learned that a gentle dove, the first day she left the nest, had succeeded in taking two foxes, one of which is old and cunning and capable all alone of shifting as many hens as any four other foxes, you would not only be amazed, but you would declare it impossible.

And that's where you would be wrong, for the thing happened here at Prato, in this very country, in these latter days, and if I can relate it to you as nicely as it took place, I have no doubt of making you laugh. Anyhow I'll try.

You know Santolo di Doppio del Quadro for one of those who are hard to deceive. He is a stoutish man with old-fashioned whiskers. He plays chess in his apron and does his own marketing. People fancy he is quite a simple man, but beware of his shoetoe! He knows his reckoning as well as another, especially when he plays cards with the ladies. He is a man of sound conscience. He would willingly help a widow who was in need of the stuff for a petticoat for a marriageable daughter, provided he was paid back the value in yarn. Taking one year with another he weaves a good deal of linen in his shop, and always has plenty of spinning to give out. When he comes unexpect - edly among a group of women seated round a fire he plants himself on the lowest stool and, if one of them drops her spindle in the ashes, he picks it up and hands it back with a low bow and then tells them some of the funniest tales you ever heard. He is a devotee of the Virgin Mary but, withall, a jolly fellow who enjoys a joke and is slow to take offense.

This man, therefore, on hearing that one of his friends was getting married, thought at once of obstructing the wedding procession, as is the custom in this town, in order to get something from the bride and then poke fun at the bridegroom, who was also a noble and gallant young man, accustomed all day long to take in others and to get himself nicely caught in his turn. He went off for one of his friends, one of those fine fellows to whom one has only to say "Come" and they come, and "Stay" and they stay, being so little accustomed to saying "No" that before coming away with you no matter where, if another arrives who wishes to take him someplace else, simply while you are getting your cloak, he will go, because he does not know how to refuse. The most serviceable man in life, if he says to one of his comrades while playing at spotted cards, "Give me the ace of denier," and the comrade hands him thirty-two, he answers, "All right." Never angry, never grumbling, never uttering an evil word, he would eat without hunger, drink without thirst, fast without there being any vigil, hear two Masses on a weekday and none on Sunday, merely for company. To give pleasure, he would sleep till midday or get up before daybreak; never eat salad in winter or drink water in summer. If you were sad, he would cheer you. If you were gay, he would make your sides split with laughing. He would sooner spend money than earn it, give than receive, oblige than ask. When he has cash, he spends it. When he has none, he lives without spending that of others. If he borrows, he gives back. If he lends, he forgets to claim it. Tell him the truth, he believes it. Tell him lies, he holds them for downright certainties. He prefers to think nothing rather than puzzle his brains, and what we must begrudge him is that he bears misfortune better than anyone else I know. In the end, he is one of the best and born to please.

Santolo, having met him, said to him, "Fallabacchio, I want us to have a bit of sport with the man who is marrying Verdespina this evening. I have found out who will be with the bride and the way they will go. I reckon we ought to get enough out of them to regale ourselves on two fat kids at their expense. And we will invite the bridegroom to the feast and have a bit of fun out of him, not half!"

"Oh! yes, yes," replied Fallabacchio, nodding his head and hugging Santolo. "Oh! we will buy two champion kids, and I will pick them myself. I will get two fat milk kids from Fagiuoli who understands such things. I will make the sauce myself, and shall boil one of the hind - quarters. I shall dress the civet with sweet marjoram and the kidneys with eggs. Oh, what a chance! How we shall make pigs of ourselves! To begin with we shall eat the livers with pepper, but no laurel, only sage!" And he jumped for joy and added, "We shall want something to drink. Where shall we go for the wine."

"You can leave that to me."

"Come on then, let's get on the job."

Thus chatting about the supper, they waited for the tidings of the bride's setting out, and then rushed off before her. Racing away, wet with sweat, and hatless, they caught the cortege near the Torre degli Scrini. Those who were accompanying the bride, seeing them from afar, said to themselves, "Here they come. What shall we do?"

The bride, quite young, as you know, and in tears at the thought of leaving home, nevertheless kept her head and replied, "Mother, let them come. I shall satisfy them, and I have thought out what to do."

Santolo and Fallabacchio had at last got up to them, and they cried out together, "Give us a tip or we shall not let you pass." But, since the folks made no reply, Fallabacchio shouted, "If you do not give us a tip I shall run away with the bride on my back."

The bride's friends looked at one another but kept silent. The chaste young bride, whose tear-stained cheeks helped the illusion, took a ring from her finger, not without much time and difficulty, and handed it to the men, saying, "Take this pledge and, for God's sake, cause no further misfortunes; but be on your guard not to lose it. It is the finest ring I have."

The merry fools, believing they had caught a fine fish, gathered their nets and went off to Antonio dei Bardi's where there were, as every evening, many gentlemen playing and otherwise passing the time. They went in laughing uproariously, and kicking up such a dust as never was, and intimating that they had just performed some wonderful cleverness, and showing the ring to any who would look. These latter, whether they knew but little about it, or to leave them in their blissful ignorance, told them the brilliant was a genuine one worth a pile of money. That their glory might be spread throughout the whole world and the high renown of so magnificent a result might be raised above the clouds, our heros re - solved to go that very night and display their trophy in the best houses of Prato and to triumph publicly over it on the next day in broad daylight.

They first visited Monna Amorrorisca, a lovely and bewitching young woman, Fallabacchio's gossip and near kin to the bride. There, with much mirth, they related the adventure and exhibited the ring at a distance as people point to the Cintola. Everyone said, "Bring it nearer." But they exclaimed, "Not likely. Do you want us to lose it?" At length, however, they let Monna Amorrorisca view it closely. As soon as she got hold of it she dis - covered that it had been fabricated at the expense of an old candlestick and that the stone was quarried in the Glass Mountains. She began to laugh and, after having kept them some time on edge, "By Gad!" she says to them, "Guard it most preciously and take care not to lose it. You would ruin Verdespina."

"The deuce! And what is it worth in your opinion?" asked Santolo.

"Indeed, the night is a bad time for valuing jewels, especially when they are of great worth, as this one is. But at a rough guess, taking into account both brass and glass, soldering, edging and chasing, it is worth not less than two quarters, perhaps three."

Santolo, assuming his serious air and snatching the ring out of her hands cried, "Oh, do you not see how she imposes on us?" But when he had the ring in his hand he did not feel quite so sure of himself. He perceived by its color and weight that he had been to catch partridges with an ox and began to puff and blow.

"What's the matter with you?" asked Fallabacchio. "Do you not see how she is jeering at us? Bitch! What a beautiful ruby! What is this I say? It is a cornelian. No, a turquoise. Anyhow, whatever it is, it is superb. I will go straightway to a goldsmith and raise a florin on it so that we can buy the kids for the day after tomorrow. What day will it fall on? It will be Saturday — they will be fat."

Without further parley, off he went to a goldsmith's shop and was assured that the ring might be a suitable present for a nursemaid in a pinch. The two friends were furious at being duped, and they swore that they would plunder the bride's trousseau and demand double the value for everything they could capture before giving it up. However the bridegroom heard of their threats, and he arranged that some of his friends should keep the two jokers out of the way until all the things were safely packed away and thus they were fooled again.

But Verdespina, ill-satisfied because of the joke was not carried further, made her intentions known to Monna Amorrorisca, and the latter, highly delighted, prepared beforehand what was to be done.

On Saturday morning Verdespina sent word to Santolo and Fallabacchio that they were to return her ring, that she would give them a gratuity, and a generous one too so that they would be able to treat themselves to a couple of kids. The fellows would have willingly believed that she wanted to make a laughing stock of them if certain folks, who had been given the hint, had not thought of whis - pering in their ears that Monna Amorrorisca had changed the ring, that they knew for certain that it was worth more than thirty crowns, and that the bridegroom was wild when he heard the story and intended to put a stop to the game at once. And, believe me, they swallowed the tale!

They went to the gossip and asked her if she had changed the ring. She first took to laughing and, while laughing, to deny it with those looks that people assume when they want to jest in saying no. They were only the more certain that the gossip had changed it and, getting very angry cried out "robber" and almost called her names — how she had them mocked by the whole town, how folks did not act in that manner, and how she must give them back the ring or take the consequences. But to irritate them both still more, she held her tongue. Fallabacchio, raising his voice even higher, cried, "Gos - sip, give us the ring. If not, I swear I will snatch your watch off you when you are at church tomorrow."

Seeing that things were going as she wished, but pretending to be affronted, Monna Amorrorisca told them she had not changed the ring to wrong them, still less to keep it, as they seemed to think, but simply to laugh over it a day or two with them, then to give it back to them. Now, since they had got angry, since they threat - ened her and made a fuss about it, she intended to treat them as they deserved. Consequently, let them not think to get back the ring unless they first paid down for two kids, and the fattest that could be found in the market this morning. Santolo and Fallabacchio, seeing her in such a rage, wished to pacify her, but all to no purpose. She left them to fight it out together and flung off saying, "Now remember what I have told you!"

The two fellows walked out quite downhearted, pondering what to do. At the same moment, the bride -

groom sent them word that he must have the ring at all costs, and they could ask whatever they liked. He wanted the matter settled at once as the joke had gone too far for his liking. Fallabacchio turned to Santolo and said, "The bridegroom is within his rights, but what the devil can we do? Let us buy the kids for the gossip. We can ask her to supper at the same time and make peace with her. Then if the bridegroom wants the ring he must pay for it. Other - wise he gets nothing."

They stuck to this resolution, went to the market, bought two fat kids, took them to the gossip and asked for the ring. She told them that she would not fail to give it to them, but not until Saturday evening, when they must come to her house and share in the feast. What she was doing with them was, she said, for their good, because she also wished to invite Verdespina and her husband, who, in this way, would feel less disinclination to settle with them generously. They told her this was a good idea, but that she ought to send word beforehand to the husband to leave them alone and not to reclaim the ring before the follow - ing evening. As to that, they might well leave it to her, she replied, for she knew quite well how to pacify the husband.

After the poor dupes departed, Monna Amorrorisca sent word to Verdespina that everything was ready for the unravelling of the plot and that she and her husband were to come to her house tomorrow evening. Verdespina re - plied that they would be there without fail.

On Sunday evening Monna Amorrorisca invited a number of girl friends and their husbands to the party, so that the joke might get discussed all over the town, and also that homage might be paid to the new-made bride. Of course, Santolo and Fallabacchio were there.

Once the supper was over, Monna Amorrorisca and Verdespina, desiring that nobody should ignore the joke played on Santolo and Fallabacchio and that the men should be thoroughly mocked, related what had hap - pened. Men and women all began to set up a clatter at the expense of the two fellows who at first seemed inclined to kick up a dust, but seeing that the more that they defended themselves the more they were laughed at, like good-natured fellows, joined in the general merriment, stating that after all it was not a miracle that they were mistaken about the value of the ring as they were not goldsmiths. But some say that Santolo did not laugh very heartily. Being more thoroughly duped, he took it more to heart.

* *
*

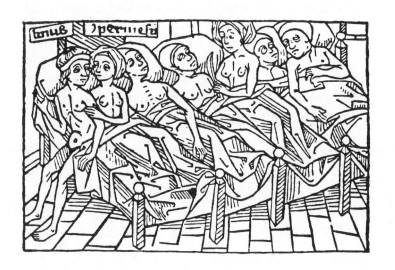

IX

THE EVEN MATCH

AS YOU MUST KNOW, THERE WAS
IN SIENA, IN THE CAMPOREGGI QUARTER — THE
TIME IS NOT SO FAR BACK BUT THAT EVERY ONE OF YOU
WILL REMEMBER IT — A CERTAIN MONNA FRANCESCA
of a pretty good family and fairly well off. She had
remained a widow with one daughter already ripe for
marriage. In fact, she got her married a few months after
to a certain Meo di Mino da Rossia who, being occupied in
the management of the magnificent Borghes' demesnes,
lived most of the time outside Siena. She also had a son
who was scarcely seven years old. Busy with bringing up
her two children and unwilling to marry again, she lived
very quietly.

In the meantime a Dominican Brother, a bachelor of
theology named Fra Timoteo, seeing she was fresh and
good-looking, cast his eyes on her. Either because of the
severe flagellations that he administered to himself, or
because of the prolonged fastings, to which he was sub -
jected, his face shone to such a degree that you could have
lighted a match on his ruddy cheeks.

The good lady thought he would be just the man for her, one who would suit her quiet situation and help her to remedy the irksome privations of widowhood. Now, whether it was from him or from her that the first ad - vances came, I really cannot say. Let it suffice for you that she became a near kin to the good Lord, and she went to confession so often and stayed so willingly at the Church of San Domenico that the people of the district proclaimed her half a saint.

While things were going on as you have just heard, the daughter, Laura, had long since discovered her mother's wisdom by many signs and, unwilling to belie that elegant proverb "The offspring of the hen must scratch the dunghill," resolved to follow her mother's example. Soon she proved so apt a pupil that, when her mother was displaying her conscience to the pious monk, she was learning from a certain Andreuolo Pannili, a lawyer, the conduct that is to be observed in the consummation of matrimony.

Now it happened that one night, while the widow was entertaining her spiritual comforter in her room, they made more noise than was wise, and the daughter figured out the nature of their devotions. Believing that now she herself needed to take no further precautions, she sent her brother to fetch their neighbor Agnesa, a friend of all true lovers, and asked her to bid her sweetheart come at once. The gentleman lost no time in putting in an appearance and, entering her room by the usual way, laid himself down by his darling in bed. But Laura, instead of arranging it so that her mother could not hear them, began to caress her lover quite as if he were her husband, saying as loudly as possible, "Oh my dear soul, you are a thousand times welcome! Oh my sweet fresh cheeks, my ruby lips, when shall I kiss you enough so as to grow weary of it, I shall not say satiated! Never, surely never, were I to kiss you till I died!" In pronouncing these words she gave him such smacks that you might have heard them a mile away. The lawyer, after he was acquainted with what was up, did not fail to do his duty, and there finally resulted such a commotion that Monna Francesca's ears tingled.

Attracted by the noise, she tiptoed to their door and discovered that they were not confining their activities to mere words. Like many another woman who busies herself with the faults of others rather than her own, she grew angry beyond all bounds and, driving the door in before her with unparalleled fury, she bounced into the room, found Laura in the bed, affronted her in such a manner that you would have said she was going to eat her up raw. Foaming with rage she squawked out, "Tell me, what's that I have been hearing you say? O Laura, Laura, is this the way virtuous girls behave? Have I taught you these things? Have I brought you up in this way? Have I grounded you on such principles that you dare to hurl this insult into my face? Have I ever set you such an example? Oh God! Whom do you take after? O my husband! How fortunate that you died and have been spared this shame. What will our relations say? What will your husband, who dotes on you so, say? You might at least have avoided such goings-on in my house and waited until your husband took you away, as he intends to do shortly. Away slut, away. Get out of my sight. You are no daughter of mine, you brazen-faced bitch! O God, I might have suspected this, had I not been blind! But alas. How could I have thought such a thing of a daughter of mine when here at this moment, though I have seen it with my own eyes, I cannot believe it. O God, my too ardent affection for Thee, the too great confidence that I had, knowing my own life, caused me to see all awry. Now I understand why the other morning at church Monna Andreoccia warned me against letting you gad about. She knew something and it only wanted this to make us the talk of the town. There then is the reason for your secret talks with that Agnesa. Yes, there it is but I'll pay you out my lady! Have I not given you a young and vigorous husband, good enough for anybody? Just you wait till he gets back. I will tell him myself what you have been doing, and he will chastise you with his own hand."

While uttering these threats and many more besides, she made as big a row as an old dame would who had lost a pen of poultry. Laura, who all the while her mother was snubbing her remained with her eyes fixed on the ground, as one wholly confused, pretending to be greatly afraid, answered her, "My dear little mamma, I accuse myself before you for having done evil and beg pardon for God's sake. I beseech you to excuse my youth, to have at the same time respect for my honor and your own, to be good enough to forgive me this time and say nothing to my husband. I swear to you on my love for him never more to do the slightest thing against your wish. This time, that God may forgive me my grievous sin, that he may withdraw me from the gates of hell and remove this thorn from my tortured flesh, I wish to make a full confession before going to sleep again. Be therefore kind enough to go to your room and fetch me that holy monk whom you are keeping locked up. It is he who shall give me absolution."

Consider how the mother felt when she heard this request and whether she regretted that she had made such a fuss about a fault of which she was now herself convicted.

At the moment when, wishing to hide her confusion, she began to mutter I know not what rigmarole altogether beside the point, it seemed to Andreuolo that now was the time to come from behind the curtain and handle the matter in legal style. So he burst in on them saying, "Monna Francesca, what is the use of all these exclama - tions? If you have discovered your daughter with a young man, she has caught you with a monk. You are both at the same game — six of one and half-a-dozen of the other. The best thing you can do is to get back to your monk while I stay here with Laura, and then we shall all four of us enjoy our love in holy accord. We shall be so cautious that no one will ever be the wiser, whereas, if you do as you say, you will throw so much meat on the fire that more than one batch of wood will be needed to cook it, and you will be the first to repent. Be wise. Take the safe road while you can and give yourself no cause for sorrow."

The poor widow knew not what to say, she was so abashed. She wanted to steal away without any further discussion. At last, feeling that she had only heard the truth she muttered, "All right, I will say no more, except that you do as you like. And I beseech you, young man, let there be no scandal." Having said there words she returned to her room.

But the young man followed her and compelled her to agree to prepare a supper for them all that very night so that they could acknowledge one another as relations and arrange that each might come to the house whenever he liked without fear of interference. The holy accord worked so well that the two women were daily more contented. It is true indeed that sometimes in the morning while talking together of their lovers' exploits, they discovered that very often the young man had allowed himself to be surpassed, and by more than one affray, by the monk, although the latter was growing old. This made Laura envious of her mother and was the cause of many quarrels with Andreuolo.

X

THE WILL

YOU SURELY KNOW THAT WE MEET
IN ALL PROFESSIONS FAR FEWER UPRIGHT MEN
THAN SORDID MEN. YOU WILL NOT THEN FIND IT VERY
STRANGE THAT THERE ARE AMONG MONKS A SMALL
number near the perfection that their rule imposes on
them, and moreover that Avarice, who reigns over all
courts, both spiritual and temporal, has claimed a little
corner within the cloisters of poor friars.

There was at Novara, a city in Lombardy, a very rich
woman named Madonna Agnesa who was left a widow
through the death of one Gaudenzio. He left her, besides
her marriage portion, which according to the customs of
these realms was considerable, immense riches, and he al -
lowed her to dispose of them freely on the condition that
she should attend to the education of the four sons he had
by her without marrying again.

Gaudenzio was hardly dead when news of the will
reached the father of the Monastery of the Brothers of
San Nazaro, since he kept a look-out for this sort of thing.
His office was to see that no pretty widow should escape
them but should gird on the cord of the blessed Saint

Francis. By becoming one of their beguines, listening to their sermons, begging their prayers for the dead, she might send them in return nice pies in the Lombardy style. Then in the process of time she should, being inflamed with burning zeal for the pious works of the blessed Fra Ginepro or some other of their saints, decide to establish in their church a chapel where they painted funny stories — such as when Saint Francis preached to the birds in the desert, or when he made the miraculous soup, or when the angel Gabriel brought him his sandals. All she need do after that was to endow it with a nice round sum so that they would be able to celebrate every year the feast of the blessed Stigmata, possessed of so many virtues, Lord my God! and to recite an office every Monday for the souls of her relations detained in the pains of Purgatory.

But for the simple reason that they cannot, because of their vow of poverty, hold so much wealth as property of the monastery, they have recently devised a scheme for possessing the wealth as chapel endowments. They think perhaps by this means to cheat our Lord in the same way as they daily cheat people. They delude themselves by thinking that God does not see the depths of their intentions and does not know not that if they act thus, it is because they are envious and jealous of those corpulent monks who, far from wandering barefoot, carry with them five pairs of pumps and do nothing but make them - selves drunk in luxurious cells. If by chance they are obliged to go outside the monastery, they jog along at their ease on a fat pony and do not tire their minds with books for fear that the knowledge they might glean from them might elate them with pride and cause them to fall away from monastic simplicity.

To return to the point, this devout father-guardian scented out the widow so well and made such a fuss around her with his sandals that she consented to become affiliated to the Third Order, and the monks got many good meals and new habits out of her. This seemed to them as yet nothing or scarcely worthwhile, and they were at her heels all day long, reminding her of the item of the chapel. But the good lady, both because she knew she would be doing wrong by robbing her sons to bestow on the monks and because she was naturally stingy, went no farther than promises.

While they were incessantly soliciting her and she feeding them on hopes, it happened that she fell danger - ously ill and sent for the father, Fra Serafino, to hear her confession. He ran to her with all speed, and as soon as he heard her confession, seeing that the vintage time had at last arrived, told her that, as an act of charity, she should think of her salvation while there was still time. She should not rely on her sons who were only waiting for her death to laugh at her. She should remember Donna Lionora Caccia, the wife of Doctor Cervagio. When she was dead there was not one of her sons who was willing to light a candle for her, not even on All Souls' Day. The amount was very little for some one as rich as she was, and both she and her relations would gain from her bequests. In short he told the tale so well that the dying woman was almost resolved to say she would and asked him to come back next day, and she would have a decision.

Meanwhile her youngest son, Agabio, having gotten a hint of what was up, told his brothers and they, to make quite sure, thought it would be well, if the monk returned, for one of them to hide under the bed and listen to the arrangement.

So on the next day Fra Serafino came back to conclude the bargain. Agabio slipped under his mother's bed and heard the monk urge her so forcibly, unfold so many arguments, quote so many doctors and put such a fright into her about Purgatory that she resolved to bequeath two hundred pounds in hard cash to build and decorate a chapel, a hundred more for the altar and ornaments, and, as a donation — provided that a feast should be celebrated in it every year and a Mass said daily — half of an undivided demesne that she owned at Camigliano, near the pillory, which was worth in all more than three thousand pounds. After agreeing on the name of the chapel and the services, the monk hurried off, and Agabio got from under the bed without his mother noticing, and he told his brothers what he had heard. Aided by a few relatives, they came to their mother and dissuaded her from such a plan.

Agabio, feeling that his mother would be satisfied to let the stream follow its natural course, thought it would be as well to get a laugh out of the father. He called aside one of the footmen and dispatched him on his mother's behalf to bid the monk not to come anymore to the house to tire her and talk over again what was settled — her sons had got to know of her scheme and planned to play him an ugly trick should he reappear. Let him nevertheless remain tranquil. She would take care that her wishes were carried out. From the moment he learned that our Lord had disposed of her, he only had to go to Ser Tomeno Alzalendina's and ask for the will and get it executed.

The footman went and delivered the message, so that Fra Serafino appeared no more. As soon as he learned, however, that Madonna Agnesa had yielded her soul to her Maker, he quickly went to Ser Tomeno and asked for the will. Ser Tomeno, advised beforehand by Agabio of what he was to do, answered him unhesitatingly that he must see Agabio who was acquainted with the provisions of the will.

Without more ado the monk called on Agabio and, after the usual expressions of sympathy, asked to see the will. Agabio made no other reply to his request except that he was greatly surprised to see him inquiring for what did not concern him and told him to mind his own business. The good father did not in any way trouble himself about this reception. He believed all the more that the will was only the more favorable to him and without further argument took himself to a certain Master Niccolo, attorney for the monastery, and asked him to deal with this affair.

Niccolo at once had Ser Tomeno summoned before the bishop's vicar and demanded a copy of the will. Tomeno, having received the summons, ran off to Agabio and told him how things stood. Agabio, who was only waiting for this, went to the vicar, who was a great friend of his, and informed him of all that had taken place up to then, as well as what he intended to do provided it had his approval. The vicar, being of course the monk's enemy in his capacity of priest, assured him that he would be very glad of it. And so the next day there came Fra Serafino and his attorney demanding that they should be shown a copy of the will.

Agabio stepped forward at this request and said, "My Lord Vicar, I am very happy to produce it in the presence of your Lordship, but on the condition that all its clauses be executed in good and due form, by all those named therein, no matter whom."

"The thing is clear," replies the vicar, "the law disposes that he who has the profits ought also to bear the charges. Therefore produce the will. Justice will have it so."

Agabio immediately pulling a large roll of paper from his pocket, handed it to a notary on the bench, telling him to read it, which he did. After reading the appointing of heirs and a few other legacies mentioned in order to aspire greater confidence in the guest, the notary came at length to the part concerning the monk, which began thus:

"Item - for the safeguard of my children's goods and the salvation of all the widows of Novara, I wish that by these same children and their own hands, there be given Fra Serafino, at present Guardian of the Convent of San Nazaro, fifty lashes, the best and heaviest they shall know how to apply, so that this monk and his equals may long remember that it is not always advisable to wish to persuade silly women without judgement, and foolish bigots, to disinherit and ruin their children for the sake of enriching chapels."

Such bursts of laughter arose from all parts of the court that the notary could not finish his reading. Do not ask me if all those present began to make a fool of the poor father who, seeing himself stuck there with shame and affront, wished to get off back to the convent and draw up a complaint to be sent to the Apostolic See.

But Agabio, seizing him by the habit and holding him fast, began to cry out, "Hold on father, whither away so fast? I am quite prepared to carry out the duties imposed on me by the will, and turning toward the vicar, without letting go of the monk, he added, "My Lord, have him stretched on the rack. I am bent on fulfilling my obliga - tion, otherwise I shall complain of your Lordship and say you have not rendered me justice."

The Vicar thought this was enough, if not too much, considering, as he ought, the dignity of the monk and the Order of the Friars Minor. He turned to Agabio and half laughing said, "Agabio, sufficient that you have shown your good will. Fra Serafino, opining that this legacy would be burdensome on the convent, refuses to accept it. Since he refuses you cannot force it on him. Let him therefore go about his business." And with the kindest words he could find, he dismissed him.

The monk, as soon as he got leave, went full of rage to the convent and remained there a long while without showing his nose, owing to his great shame. He never again exhorted widows to bequeath their goods to chapels, especially if they had grown-up sons capable of holding him up to ridicule. Yet, the Vicar repented since the joke cost him more than five hundred florins.

* *
*

BIBLIOGRAPHY

EDITIONS

Alcune prose scelte. Venice: Alvisopoli, 1838.
"Gli apologhi," in *Tesoro della prosa italiana.* Eugenio Alberi, ed. Florence, 1841.
L'Asino d'oro. Adriano Seroni, ed. Rome: Columbo, 1943.
Le belezze le lodi, gli amori & i costumi delle donne. Venice: Barezzi, 1622.
Commedie cioe La trinutia e I Lucidi. Venice: G. Giolito de' Ferrari, 1561.
Commedie con annotazioni. Trieste: Lloyd Austriaco, 1858.
Consigli de gli animali. Venice: Barezzi, 1622.
I discoursi delle belezze delle donne. Rome: Perino, 1891.
Due novelle. Livorno: F. Vigo, 1869.
"I Lucidi," in *Tressino.* Giovanni Giorgio. Bologna: Forni, 1974.
I Lucidi commedia. Florence: Bernardo Giunnti, 1549.
I Lucidi commedia. Venice: G. Giolito de' Ferrari, 1560.
I Lucidi commedia. Florence: F. Giunti, 1595.
I Lucidi commedia. Venice: Bartholomeo Carampello, 1597.
Novelle. Giuseppe Lipparini, ed. Rome: Formiggini, 1923.
Novelle. Adriano Seroni, ed. Milan: Bompiani, 1944.
Novelle. Eugenio Ragni, ed. Milan: G. Salerno, 1971.
Novelle di Agnolo Firenzuola. Olindo Guerrini, ed. Florence: G. Barrbèra, 1886.
Delle opere di M. Agnolo Firenzuola, Fiorentino. Pier Luigi Fantini, ed. Florence: 1723.
Opere. Brunone Bianchi, ed. 2 vols. Florence: Le Monnier, 1816. Reprint ed., Naples: F. Giannini, 1864.

Opere. Adriano Seroni, ed. Florence: Sansoni, 1958.
Opere di Agnolo Firenzuola. B. Bianchi, ed. Florence: Le Monnier, 1848.
Opere di Messer Agnolo Firenzuola. Lorenzo Scala and Pier Luigi Fantini, eds. Florence, 1763-66.
Opere di Messer Agnolo Firenzuola. Pisa: N. Capuro, 1816.
Opere di Messer Agnolo Firenzuola, Fiorentino. 5 vols. Milan: Società tipografica de' classici italiani, 1802.
Opere scelte. G. Fatini, ed. Turin, 1957.
La prima veste de' Discorsi degli animali. Pavia: G. Torri, 1822.
La prima veste de' Discorsi degli animali. Milan: Molina, 1833.
La prima veste dei Discorsi degli animali e altre prose. Pierluigi Donini, ed. Rome: G.B. Paravia, 1876.
Prose. Florence: I. Giunti, 1562.
Prose. Florence: Barbera, 1892.
Prose di M. Agnolo Firenzuola, Fiorentino. Florence: B. Giunti, 1548.
Prose di M. Agnolo Firenzuola Fiorentino. Florence: L. Torrentino, 1552.
Prose purgate ed annotate. Celestino Durando, ed. Turin: Libreria Salesiana, 1904.
Prose scelte. Florence: Poligrafia, 1847.
Prose scelte. Adriano Seroni, ed. Florence: Sansoni, 1957.
Prose scelte e annotate. Severino Ferrari, ed. Florence: Sansoni, 1895. Reprint, 1915, 1938.
Ragionamenti. Lodovico Domenichi, ed. Venice: Griffio, 1552.
Ragionalenti d'amore e altri scritti. Bartolomeo Rossetti, ed. Rome: Avancini & Torraca, 1966.
Le Rime di M. Agnolo Firenzuola, Fiorentino. Florence: B. Giunti, 1549.
Scritti scelti. Enrico Mastica, ed. Turin: E. Loescher, 1890.
La Trinutia. Venice: G. Griffio, 1552.
La Trinutia. Florence: F. Giunti, 1593.
La Trinutia. Delmo Maestri, ed. Turin: Einaudi, 1970.

TRANSLATIONS

The Bawdy Tales of Firenzuola. Jules Griffon, trans. Covina, CA: Collectors Publications, 1967.
"The Friar of Novara" in *Great Short Stories of the World*. B.H. Clark, ed. New York: McBride & Co., 1929.

"Novels," in *Italian Novelists*. Thomas Roscoe, ed. Vol. 2. London: W. Simpkin & R. Marshall, 1836.

Of the Beauty of Women. Clara Bell, trans. London: J.R. Osgood, McIlvaine & Co., 1892.

The Tales of Firenzuola. Anon. trans. Paris: Liseux, 1889.

The Tales of Firenzuola. Anon. trans. New York: Firenzuola Society, 1929.

The Tales of Firenzuola. New York: Valhalla Books, 1964.

SECONDARY WORKS

Angeli, Siro. "Le commedie di Agnolo Firenzuola," *Revista italiana del dramma* 1 (1940): 209-19.

Ciofardini, Emanuele. "Agnolo Firenzuola," *Rivisti d'Italia* 15 (1912): 3-46, 881-946.

Fatini, G. *Agnolo Firenzuola*. Milan: Marzorati, 1961.

—. *Agnolo Firenzuola e la borghesia letterata del Rinascimento*. Cortona, 1907.

—. "Nel IV centenario della morte di Agnolo Firenzuola," *La Rinascità* 6 (1943).

—. "Per un' edizione critica delle opere di Agnolo Firenzuola," *Studi di filologia italiana* 14 (1956): 21-175.

Novelle del Cinquecento. Second ed. Giambattista Salinari, ed. Turin: Società editrice subalpina, 1976.

Porcelli, Bruno. *La novella del Cinquecento*. Rome: Laterza, 1973.

Rossi, M. "L'Asino d'oro" *di Agnolo Firenzuola*. Città di Castello, 1901.

Segre, C. "Edonismo linguistico nel Cinquecento," *Giornale storico della letteratura italiana* 130 (1953): 145-77.

—. *Lingua, stile e società*. Milan, 1963.

Seroni, Adriano. *Apologia di Laura, ed altri saggi*. Milan: Bompiani, 1948.

—. *Bibliografia essenziale delle opere del Firenzuola*. Florence: Sansoni, 1957.

* *
*

This Book Was Completed on February 20, 1987
at Italica Press, New York, New York and
Set in Times Roman. It Was Printed
on 55 lb Glatfelter Natural Paper
with a Smyth-Sewn Binding by
McNaughton & Gunn,
Saline, MI
U. S. A.

* *